Avery Aarons believes it's fate that she will die by the hand of a criminal. As a child, she hid in a cupboard while men ransacked their home. In college, she met with an attacker walking home on campus. After that, going into law enforcement is her only path to protect herself and others who can't. She's never felt so empowered, until she ends up in the wrong place without backup.

When Jess Monet attends a CPR refresher course and runs into the sexy brown-eyed officer his special ops team helped out, he's just as impressed this time around. He must admit, Avery's got some pretty damn good moves on the CPR dummy too, though Jess has had his fill of rejection lately and is reluctant to pursue more than a friendship with the tough, beautiful woman. He also knows she's completely right for him.

While on a short hiatus from her job due to an investigation, Avery has no idea what to do with her time. Spending it with the hunky special ops man is driving her to distraction, though, and she wishes he'd just make a move. Preferably one that lands them both naked in bed. Too soon fate comes after her again, and this time she's sure it's the end for her. But Jess isn't about to let anything happen to the woman he's growing too fond of to deny... the only woman who can rescue him right back.

More in this series:

TARGET IN RANGE

by

Em Petrova

Prologue

The wind howled through the trees outside Avery's bedroom window, but it didn't mask the thump of boots and slamming of doors.

Somebody was in the house.

Why, oh why had she said she was too old for a babysitter? Her parents wouldn't be home for hours from their cards night with friends, and she knew those rough, low voices coming from the front of the house did not belong to her parents.

She had woken the second she heard the back door. Nobody used the back, and at that moment, she knew what was going on.

Robbers had come, and she was alone. Helpless.

Her heart pounded in her ears and filled her chest, slamming until it hurt and she felt it all the way up into her teeth. Her hands were icy, but there was no turning over and cuddling beneath her Hello Kitty quilts.

She had to hide.

The men weren't bothering to be quiet—they thought the house was empty. They were coming down the hall.

"Find the bedroom. Women always have jewelry." One man's voice jolted her with how close it was to her door.

"Might be a gun there too. I'd like another to add to my collection."

"Yeah, gotta protect against people like you."

The coarse words barely registered in Avery's head. She rolled out of bed to her knees. Thank goodness she had carpet and made no sound. But she couldn't move either—she was frozen in fear, her stare locked on the door, waiting for it to burst inward and the evil men to look her in the eyes.

She peered through the strands of her brown hair. They wavered in front of her vision, because she was shaking.

One more heavy footstep, just outside her door.

She scrambled up and lunged toward her closet.

No, it was always the first place robbers looked. She needed another hiding spot.

Avery was a reader, and for her tenth birthday, her daddy had construction workers come in and build her a book nook around her window with a seat underneath. Her momma had sewn her a plump cushion, and Avery spent hours curled up there reading every chance she got.

Shelves surrounded the window, all packed with her favorite mysteries and books about girls winning championships for riding horses. Recently, her teacher had loaned her the first book of a series about

2

girls in middle school, and Avery was captivated by all the changes that would take place in her future, namely getting boobs and liking boys.

Under the window seat was an empty cupboard, not yet filled with books, but Avery had shoved some old sneakers and dirty clothes in there when her momma told her to clean her room. It was big enough to hide in.

Shuffling on hands and knees as fast as she could, she reached the cupboard and yanked open the door. Diving inside head-first, she held her breath. Her lungs burned and her head swam. She took a shallow breath and let it trickle out slowly as she drew the door shut.

Too late, she realized she might not be able to open the cupboard door from the inside and could be trapped in here without much air and a pair of dirty old sneakers stuffed in the corner until her parents came home.

On the other side of the wall in her parents' room, she heard drawers opening and things hitting the floor as they were tossed about. Ransacked, was the word, she'd read once. Until now, she hadn't totally pictured what it meant.

Pressing a hand over her drumming heart, she strained to listen. She heard something smash, probably the pretty lamp with flowers her momma liked so much.

Then one man said, "Found it."

"Looks like a .38 Special."

"Yeah, bullets too. Now find the jewelry and we can get outta here."

Avery slumped in the cupboard, nose smashed against the wood while tears silently rolled down her cheeks. *Please don't let my mom and dad come home till they're gone. Please don't' let them come for me too.*

When the steps moved out of her parents' room next door to hers, she squeezed her eyes shut and mentally begged them not to come in. Her door burst inward, smashing off the wall.

"Just a kid's room. Nothin' here."

The steps moved on.

She focused on the sound of their steps, tracking them through the rest of the house, and finally heard nothing. Her heart wouldn't slow, and she was terrified to open the cupboard door to find the men staring at her, so she stayed hidden until she heard her father's shouts and her mother's shrill cry.

It was a long time before she could sleep in her own bed again.

Chapter One

Jess brought his energy drink to his lips and sipped. It was his second of the afternoon, and he'd pay for it by fucking up his sleep schedule for a week, but staying alert was more important than his future sleep habits.

He'd just spent eighteen hours hunting down a homegrown terrorist through back country Texas and into Oklahoma. They'd ranged all over, tracking the lone wolf who seemed to have no alliance to country or ties to any one group which would help Ranger Ops locate him.

Then when they had, they'd been surprised to find he wasn't operating alone, after all. Good thing they knew how to think on the fly, because being outnumbered in men and weapons hadn't mattered when up against their tactics and skills.

Though their Hail-Mary maneuver had gotten Jess some bruised ribs when he'd taken two rounds in the Kevlar vest, they'd been victorious.

But after putting out that dumpster fire, he'd come home and been handed this mess. He stared at the three computer monitors in front of him, each bearing a man's photo and what looked like a list of terroristic achievements underneath.

How Jess had moved into the role of special forces intelligence analyst on the side was a story to tell down at the bar—not that he could tell a single soul. They'd all think he'd had one too many whiskey chasers if he said his colonel in an elite division of Homeland Security had given Jess a phone call from a terrorist one night, and Jess had handled it well enough to continue with the work.

Gathering intel on a spy who fed information to various terrorist groups around the world took more of Jess's strength and focus than hand-to-hand combat with any enemy.

He studied the face on the first monitor. Andres Moreno didn't look different from any man you'd see on a city street, in a church pew or seated at the next table in a restaurant. He was mid-thirties, clean-cut and wore small wire glasses that gave him a studious look. But that was where the good-guy resemblance ended.

Under his photo, his rap sheet went on and on. He'd provided intelligence resulting in more bombings and attacks than the other two men filling Jess's computer screens.

The next was Edgar Ortiz, and the man Moreno was speaking to currently. He had a neck like a bull and eyes without any semblance of kindness in the black depths. He'd been convicted twice and served time in prison. But that hadn't stopped him from

6

continuing on his quest to control the politicians of Mexico City through intimidation and the ever-present threat of violence.

Jess adjusted his headset and focused more on the conversation taking place between the two men.

Over the past few months, he'd heard this suspect's voice so much he felt as if he knew the guy better than his own brothers. He hadn't spoken to the three of them in months. They were busy, he was busy. What little free time he had, he was eavesdropping on this motherfucker.

He sighed and made a note of something, translating it from the Spanish he'd just heard to English for his superior officers. After he got the intel he needed from this asshole, Homeland Security would strike, and Ranger Ops would likely be heading the operation.

The man's inflection changed, and Jess perked up. His son was in the room, and he was speaking to the kid.

May I go outside and play with Esteban?

It's getting late. Nearly time for supper.

Please, Papa? Just ten minutes.

Ten will turn to half an hour and then I will be out after dark searching for my son. You know the rules, Brayan.

Oh all right, Papa.

Mijo. Come here and let me give you a hug. Then run into the kitchen and tell Juanita that you can spoil your supper with a sweet.

Really? Thanks!

Jess compressed his lips. He wouldn't scribble this exchange in his notes—what he was listening for were details outside of Andres Moreno's personal life. The man had a son and a daughter, though Jess rarely heard him speak to the girl. He also had a wife, who had 'suddenly died.' In US terms, she'd had several Xanaxes with her bottle of tequila, but knowing Moreno's world, Jess questioned if she had been killed.

This was all speculation, of course. Something had to keep his mind busy during the long, dull hours of listening to Moreno talk about nothing.

His intel training had taught him to pick out things that sounded and seemed normal as well. Often intel was hidden, embedded in regular conversations. Just about every government agency had had reason to suspect well-kept secrets were shared right under their noses, though as of yet no one had been able to pin down exactly when, where, or with who. The only common denominator was Moreno, which is why Homeland Security had had him on their radar for a year, but Jess had only been brought in a few months ago to do his part.

He yawned so wide his jaw cracked—the energy drink hadn't kicked in yet. He took another sip and blinked at his surroundings.

His muscles were screaming from sitting still so long, and his bruised ribs would cause problems when trying to sleep, but that didn't matter because he couldn't sleep now anyway.

The talk went on between Moreno and yet another friend—his fourth this afternoon. The guy's photo flipped onto Jess's screen.

Man, this asshole's chattier than a damn woman.

The mundane stuff often held hidden meaning, though, so Jess listened harder.

Our team isn't doing well this season...

When I drove into the city, there was road construction and many stops...

Hey, Papa, Juanita told me I mustn't ruin my dinner with sweets unless you do as well. She gave me a torta de tres leches for you, too.

Jess translated that to a triple milk cake, and his stomach growled despite the fact he had no clue how the pastry would taste. He was, however, thinking of one of his momma's treats she made him and his brothers when they were young. Apple dumplin's were always their favorite, and they'd ask for them every chance they got.

Apple dumplin's with ice cream, he thought.

The familiar voice of Moreno's son projected into Jess's ear. *I love you, Papa.*

Love you too, son.

Since his own father had taken off before he could remember, Jess heard exchanges such as this and marveled that there were father-son relationships like it. Closest he came was a punch in the shoulder from his older brother Jeremy.

He listened another few minutes with nothing in particular standing out to him as important. When the call between Moreno and his friend ended, Jess pulled off his headphones and swiped a hand over his face. Now that they were finished up, the energy drink was kicking in, his body energized with caffeine just in time to hit the sack.

He shot off a text to Colonel Downs.

All is dark.

Downs returned it almost immediately. *Knock off. Talk to you tomorrow.*

Jess set aside his headphones and got off his chair. Taking a few steps to his window, he looked out into the street where he lived. Everything was still outside, his neighbors home from work and their cars tucked neatly away in their garages. They were all indoors, making dinner for their families.

He didn't have one of those to claim.

He was no longer tired.

Hell, if he wasn't looking out the window, he'd have no damn clue what time of day it was. His body said it was time for bed, but the caffeine held his eyelids open.

It's the time when a man turns to his lover and burns off his insomnia on pleasuring her.

Except there was no lover either.

10

If he had any luck with women, it was bad luck. The guys in Ranger Ops razzed him that he'd been dumped more than their loads of dirty laundry.

Jess was resigned to the fact that he was utterly dump-able. If he danced all night with a woman, he'd text her later, only to learn she was back with her ex. Hell, his last long-term girlfriend kept hounding him to move in together but when he agreed and they started looking at apartments, she'd run off with the realtor showing them to her.

His buddy and fellow Ranger Ops teammate Cavanagh, or Cav, said that women wanted to be treated like crap and then they'd be all over Jess, but he thought that was bullshit too.

He was thirty-six years old, had never been married and had nobody to share his bed on a long night when he was pumped full of too much caffeine.

Resigned with his lot in life, he let out a sigh and moved away from the window. He slowly lowered himself onto the sofa, careful of his ribs, and switched on the TV to watch the football highlights from games he always missed because he was working.

Meanwhile, his mind was wide awake, working over the fact that when Ranger Ops finally got enough intel to strike Moreno, the man's son would be orphaned.

Now *that* was the kind of shit that kept a man up at night.

11

* * * * *

Avery switched her shopping bags to one hand and reached inside her purse for her car keys. As she withdrew them, she glanced up over the hood of her car and across the parking lot. The big overhead lamps cast circles of light onto the asphalt, but off to the side in the shadows, she saw something that had her looking twice.

Quickly, she opened her car and tossed the bags on the seat. Then she turned to look again.

An altercation between a man and woman. He appeared to be shoving her against the side of his truck. She slipped away, and he grabbed her back. There was a thudding noise when her spine hit the metal.

Hell. She'd been called to enough of these cases along with her partner on the police force, Reggie. There was a domestic taking place right here at the grocery store. But Avery was off duty and should call for —

The man raised his arm and backhanded the woman. She crumpled.

Avery took off running, hand on the butt of the concealed weapon she'd carried since she became legal age… and right after she'd been attacked on her college campus.

She ran swiftly and silently, her sneakers barely making noise on the hot asphalt. She crouched behind the truck just as the woman let out a muffled scream.

Straightening, she walked around the car, hand still on her lower back where her weapon nestled. "Hey! Get your hands off her," she called out.

The guy whipped around. The woman collapsed against the truck and scrabbled to open the door in attempt to get away from him.

"Who the hell're you? Get out of here, woman!" He spat at Avery.

"Step out from around the truck, and get your hands where I can see them," Avery shouted back.

"Fuck you, lady. Goddamn women think they own me." He drove a fist into the truck door. "Kayla, get outta the truck now!"

"Sir, step away from the truck!" Avery commanded in the same forceful tone. Under her fingers, the warm steel of her pistol gave her confidence.

"Kayla, get out!" he bellowed. Across the lot, other store patrons ran to their cars.

Avery heard the click of the truck door locks, but just then the guy went for his waistband.

He has a weapon.

She pulled her own.

His eyes were wild.

He made a sharp move, and Avery took the shot.

Without blinking. Without thinking.

Inside the truck, the woman shrieked and then jumped out. "You shot him! You shot my boyfriend!"

Avery reached for her cell to call for that backup—something she should have done before running to the scene.

Adrenaline coursed through her, but she kept her tone calm as she placed the call for the police and medical rescue.

The woman hovered over her man, crying through her eye that was swelling shut, screaming for him to get up and they could just go home and work things out.

"Lady, let me see if I can help him." Avery dropped to her knees, scanning the shadows for sight of the weapon he'd been about to pull on her.

"You shot him! You can't help him now!"

Avery placed a hand on her shoulder and pushed her back so she could inspect the man.

Her shot was true. She registered this in a detached way, her stomach stone cold as she saw the blood on the man had slowed to a trickle. He was still alive, but just barely clinging on.

In the distance, the wail of sirens signaled a rapid approach. Avery reached for the man, and the woman threw her body across him. With a calm she mustered from a deep well, Avery touched the woman's shoulder again gently. "Honey, let me see if I can help your boyfriend. The ambulance is on its way, and we'll get you checked out too."

"I don't need any help! Bobby! Bobby, are you okay? Get up and we'll go home, baby."

The initial punch of adrenaline was fading, leaving behind the emotion Avery hated dealing with after an altercation.

Right now, she needed to find that weapon and get it away from the man in case he roused enough energy to take a shot at her — or his girlfriend did.

Pushing the woman back again, Avery felt the man's sides. Nothing. Maybe the gun was underneath him. He'd fallen on it.

Careful not to move him, she risked running her fingers under his sides.

The sirens grew louder, and the flashing lights hit the asphalt. Avery reached for the man's neck to feel for a pulse. It was there, though faint, just the slightest tremor beneath her fingertips.

"My boyfriend! Help my boyfriend! She shot him!"

Avery's heart gave a hard lurch against her ribs, and a sickening dread spread through her. What if there wasn't a gun under the assailant?

But no — he'd made a move for it. She'd done what any officer would have done. Her training had kicked in, and she'd only protected herself and possibly the girlfriend.

"Please move aside." The medics were on the scene and in her face.

One of the beat cops she knew pretty well was right behind. He took a good look at her face and said, "Jesus, Aarons. What happened?"

Relief washed through her, and she found her brass balls once again. "There was a domestic. He was throwing her around and hit her."

"You're off duty."

"Yes."

"Before you move that man, I need to take photos," her fellow officer, Feeland, said to the medics.

"You're going to have to take them while we administer CPR." They were already going at it, performing chest compressions and rescue breathing with the bag.

Avery looked away, the bile rising to tickle the back of her throat.

Someone had their arm around the girlfriend, leading her away from the scene, and she realized it was Feeland's partner, Callahan.

Everything around her seemed to be moving in slow motion, even the lights from the vehicles swirling across the parking lot.

"What the hell were you doing here, Aarons?" Feeland barked out.

"Getting groceries. My car's parked over there." She waved a hand, and he followed the path. "I heard them arguing and saw him shove her against the truck. Then he hit her, and I ran toward them to put a stop to it."

"And you shot an unarmed man."

16

She blinked. "I shot a man after he went for his weapon."

"Yeah, well, he's unarmed."

Jesus Christ.

It had finally happened.

What she'd feared from the very start of her career in law enforcement. She had finally allowed her own personal experiences—the home robbery when she was a child and the campus attack that had left her bruised and bleeding, but not raped, thank God—to overwhelm her choices.

No, that wasn't true. She shoved back at the thoughts rushing her mind, piling up like an accident on the interstate. She had acted out of necessity.

"He went for his weapon."

"He's not armed," Feeland told her again.

"He reached for his waistband."

Feeland's eyes took on an expression of understanding. "Yeah, I've seen that myself a time or two. Shit, Aarons. You couldn't have been in a worse part of the parking lot. I'm not sure the cameras even reach this far. If there's footage at all, it's going to be crap. Come back to the station with me. We need to tell your side of the story."

A second and third cruiser arrived on the scene, and while they handled the details of the shooting as well as the girlfriend, Avery went with Feeland and Callahan. Sitting in the back of the cruiser was strange enough without knowing what was coming.

She was an off-duty cop who'd just shot an unarmed man. The press would have a heyday with this, and she'd seen officers suspended for stupider things.

A report came through the radio.

"Fuck. The guy just coded on the way to the hospital," Callahan said from the passenger's seat. He threw her a look over his shoulder.

She dropped her face into her hands and tried to keep breathing. Her world might be crashing down, but she had just cause, a reason to discharge her weapon. Any officer in the city would have done the same.

Her mind rolled back the years to her childhood. That feeling of helplessness and terror when the robbers had entered her home had lived with her a long time. Even after a year of counseling, she'd still relived the event in dreams.

Then in college, walking home after a late class, she'd been attacked. The guy was big, heavy, and stunk of pot and beer. As he'd pushed his way between her legs and tore her pants downward, she'd gotten a hand free from his grip long enough to stab him with her pen.

She'd dragged herself off the ground and run for her life. They'd never found her attacker, but no big surprise there. Nobody showed up at the campus medical station for treatment of a stab wound administered by a pen.

But from that day forward, Avery's path in life had changed. She dumped her communications major and took up police science. She'd joined the ROTC and learned everything she could about self-protection and overpowering somebody larger than her.

She would not be a victim again.

Now, she'd dropped right back in that damn place... she was the girl with no hope. They'd strip her badge.

No, she couldn't believe that—wouldn't. Her chief would stand up for her, and so would her partner Reggie. She had people on her side, and there *would* be camera footage from the grocery store. Even if it was dim, there were ways to improve the quality and make out things, such as a man going for his waistband.

Dammit. She could have sworn he was reaching for a weapon. Anybody would, she told herself again.

Two hours later, she was informed that the victim was stabilized and his girlfriend taken to a center for domestic abuse.

Lines bracketed the chief's mouth when he took Avery's badge and suspended her for thirty days barring an internal review.

Her perfect takedown record was lost, relinquished to an officer nobody seemed to like, not that it was a popularity contest. Still, it stung her even more to know one split second had dropped her several rungs in the ladder she'd fought so hard to climb.

When she was driven back to her car at the grocery store, she found her frozen items had melted all over the seat. The perfect end to her day.

Chapter Two

Jess got out of his truck, rubbing at the stiff muscles in the back of his neck, trying to loosen them. Knotted from being hunched over in his desk chair, listening intently to hours of phone conversations between Moreno and half a dozen other men, his body wasn't letting Jess forget the abuse it'd suffered. At least the ribs were healing.

He was also dragging from little sleep—again. The story of his life these days. He couldn't remember a time he woke feeling rested. His easy, breezy carefree days had vanished the minute he became a state trooper years ago. Then came the Texas Rangers, a short-lived stint he'd enjoyed very much. And finally, being recruited to the Ranger Ops team.

With each position, his stress doubled at the very least. Some days it was a hell of a lot more than double. He was well aware he'd lost that ephemeral balance in his life with work owning him more and more. He just had no damn clue how to remedy it.

Part of him said all he needed was a beautiful woman in his bed, but that would only end in more stress if he liked her, because it meant she'd break it off, and he'd be stuck feeling like an ass all over again.

Pushing out a sigh, he entered the door of the fire station where the CPR course was taking place. He could think of at least five other things he should be doing right now. Hell, he'd prefer dealing with the heap of smelly laundry in the corner of his bedroom to being certified in CPR for what—the tenth time? If only these people knew he'd performed it just last week to save a shooting victim, they'd sign the certificate and let Jess walk out the door.

He scanned the room and held back another sigh.

Yeah, typical class, right down to the small table set up in the corner. Afterward, cups of semi-warm juice and a platter of cookies would appear there.

He didn't release the sigh lingering at the back of his throat, because at that moment, an old buddy of his walked up and held out a hand.

"Missouri," Jess said with real affection for the guy who'd been on more than one accident scene with him back in the day. He gripped his hand.

"Jess, you son-of-a-bitch. Haven't seen you for ages. Where ya been?" Missouri wasn't his real name, but Jess's brain was too foggy to recall his real one.

"You know—just work and more work."

"Yeah, I do know. I was out till 4:00 a.m. on a three-alarm night before last. Still haven't caught up on sleep."

"Know the feeling."

The woman leading the class spoke from the front of the room, gaining their attention. As people parted from their small conversation groups, Jess caught sight of a woman. Warm brown hair tied back at the nape, the ends curling between her shoulder blades.

She was fit, with muscular thighs and an ass you could bounce the proverbial quarter off—though he could think of a few other things he'd prefer to bounce off it. And those black stretchy pants must have been made by a man, because only somebody who could appreciate how a woman looked in them could have designed such a thing.

She turned her head a bit, giving him a hint of her cheekbone and jaw. Not enough to say her face was just as attractive as the rest of her body, but enough to gain Jess's interest.

With half an ear on the speaker, he continued to study her. She had a way of standing—legs braced apart—that placed her, in his mind, as a woman who was ready for action. He was betting on her being a warden at the women's prison.

As he looked on, she brushed a tendril of hair back to reveal the shell of her ear, sporting a tiny silver hoop.

His stare latched onto it.

Suddenly, everybody was splitting into groups, and Jess jolted. Missouri nudged him. "Zoned out a minute there, didn't ya?"

"Musta," he answered.

The rescue dummies were stacked in a corner, and everyone started pulling them down and laying them out on the floor. When the woman reached for one, Jess admired the way her thigh muscles tensed in those pants. Then she turned with the dummy in her arms, and he got a look at her face.

Eyes on his, deep brown and almond-shaped, her nose a perfect upturned button and lips so full all he could think about was how she'd use them.

She dropped her gaze and moved to lay out the dummy in a spot toward the back of the room.

He followed her. "Mind if we partner up?" he asked.

"Suit yourself." She lifted a shoulder and let it fall in a nonchalant shrug that would have him backing off in a hurry any other time. But for whatever reason, he didn't care if she tried to blow him off. He just wanted to spend an hour watching her.

They knelt on the floor over their dummy, and the instructor droned on about what to do if they came across a person who was unconscious.

"I'm Jess Monet," he said, low.

She gave him a look, one he'd be tempted to peg as disinterested, unfeeling even. But as he scanned her posture more closely, what he sensed was calm as she answered with, "Avery Aarons."

Oh shit. He knew that name. She'd been in the newspaper recently. She was the cop who'd been suspended pending internal review due to shooting a

24

man who was beating up his girlfriend in a grocery store parking lot. Of course, the man's family was pressing charges, because he was still in critical condition, days after the event.

Her shot had been perfectly placed.

All this ran through his mind in a blink, and he kept it off his face. "Nice to meet you."

She didn't respond, just eyed him before turning her attention to the instructor.

Jess hated to see her go down for doing her job, even if she had been off duty, but unfortunately it was a hazard of walking the beat. You got yourself into dirty shit, were in the wrong place at the wrong time, without backup and stuck making your own judgment call. Sometimes it backfired on you.

"You check your victim to see if he's choking," the instructor said. They watched a quick video on it, and then they were told to check their own victim.

Avery's stare centered on Jess. "You want to check first?"

"Sure."

He made an automatic sweep of the dummy, his awareness on Avery. She tucked a hair behind her ear again, and damn if he wasn't thinking about batting that little silver hoop with his tongue.

His jeans were becoming a bit tight in his kneeling position, and he shifted to ease himself.

When he was finished checking the dummy, he sat back on his haunches. "Your turn."

Avery's ponytail swung forward over her shoulder as she bent to listen for breaths and felt for a pulse.

The class continued on, with them learning the basics for recertification. Jess was glad he could do this in his sleep, because it afforded him time to study Avery.

"So you come here often?" he asked as an icebreaker joke.

She looked up and gave him a ghost of a smile. "Every so often," she responded.

"Me too. What a coincidence."

Her smile stretched and then fell away as she did what the instructor asked of them. They were shown another video on the number of breaths to administer in ratio to chest compressions. When it was their turn to try the skill, he gave Avery a wave.

"You go on."

She maneuvered into position, and the instructor appeared next to them. "Can you tell me the steps before you begin?" she asked Avery.

She glanced up, her pretty face blank. Just as quickly as she seemed to forget, she remembered what to do.

"First you recognize the emergency." She tapped on the victim and shouted for him to respond.

The instructor nodded.

"Then you call EMS. After that, you…"

A long second passed. She threw a look at Jess. The moment stretched on with Jess excruciatingly aware of Avery's nerves hitting full force. Whether it was being put on the spot or the ordeal she was going through at work with the investigation, he didn't know, but his inner rescuer kicked in.

He caught her eye and took an exaggerated breath, making sure his chest rose and fell for her to see.

"You check for breathing," she said, color flooding her cheeks.

"Good, keep going with that." The instructor moved away to the next party.

"Oh God," Avery said, face blanching white now. "Thank you for reminding me of the order. I completely blanked out there for a second."

"It happens. You all right? Want to grab a drink of water or something?"

"Do they have water?"

"It's a fire station—they've gotta have some, right?"

His flippant remark made her chuckle, and suddenly the color was normal in her face again. He smiled at her, and she continued the steps, executing them perfectly.

When it came time for her to perform rescue breathing, his stare lingered agonizingly on her lips pressed over the dummy's. Those two breaths she delivered had never looked so hot from any of his other partners.

Damn. That's one lucky dummy.

* * * * *

Avery's brain had turned into a traffic jam. Packed with the language of the investigation and the questions she was still trying to find answers to. Remembering the steps of CPR was the furthest thing from her mind.

Then add in a hot man sitting a foot away from her, watching her every move, and she could hardly think straight.

Jess — even his name was hot. All lean muscle and bulky shoulders, he definitely fit the image of a firefighter or some similar profession. The black shirt he wore lent him a more dangerous look, as if the shadow darkening his chiseled jaw wasn't enough. He wore a gold cross around his neck. And his jeans straining across carved thighs was... distracting to say the least.

More thoughts piling up in her brain.

Noticing guys wasn't a thing for her, because in general, men were just buddies.

Of course, she'd never run across a guy who looked like Jess.

Clearly, her review needed to be resolved fast so she could return to work.

She shot Jess a look. Damn, he really was good-looking and not in one of those muscle-bound jerk ways.

He probably thought her a twit after she'd blanked on those steps while the instructor was looming over her. But he'd helped her out by giving her a hint. After class, she'd be sure to thank him.

He gave her a smile as he positioned his hands over the rescue dummy's chest. When he delivered compressions, it was impossible for Avery not to soak in the appearance of those hands.

Long fingers, broad palms. His fingertips roughened by calluses, and veins snaked over the backs of his hands and up his forearms. Following one, she found it disappeared into a bulging biceps muscle.

Watching him mindlessly perform CPR on their victim, she realized this class was difficult for her after what she'd done the other night.

Get yourself together, she told herself for the hundredth time since she'd shot that man.

Sure, she'd shot people before—the job called for it. Most people she'd apprehended had thrown down weapons or given themselves up, and things hadn't gone that far. Then this one wasn't even armed…

She pushed out a heavy sigh.

Jess's gaze fell over her. "You okay?"

She nodded. But she wasn't, not really. Damn the counselor from her youth who had given her such an awareness of her feelings, of owning them. Now when she wanted to forget and shove them all down into a locked vault, she couldn't.

No, she wasn't okay. She felt like a hot mess and was sure Jess must think her an idiot. She had to focus and get through the certification so she could go off and be alone. Later, she'd attend another kickboxing class. While it left her sore, she had worked out some of her anger.

The instructor interrupted the activity in the room and halted Avery's thoughts. "All right, since everybody's had ample time for practice, are you ready for the testing?"

Jess sat back on his haunches again, attention fixed on the front of the room where the instructor stood. When he turned his head to look at Avery, he caught her staring at him.

He offered a smile that tipped up on one side more than the other. "Are you ready?"

"Yes."

"Then let's go first and get it over with so we can get outta here."

She nodded.

In seconds, Jess had the instructor convinced to start the testing at the back of the room. Several people at the front groaned in response, and his eyes twinkled when he threw Avery another smile.

"Let's see what you can do," the instructor said, standing over them.

"Ladies first." Jess waved a hand.

She engaged her brain and began the rescue. After the first two steps, her mind blanked out once more.

Dammit. Think!

Jess made a slight movement, and it came rushing back.

Fingers tingling with relief, she proceeded through the rest of the rescue without fault. Then it was Jess's turn. She moved aside to watch.

Each movement was sure and confident. When he bent to demonstrate mouth-to-mouth breathing, he actually threw her a cocky side grin before closing his lips over the protective barrier they used on the dummies.

Next, he had to show the instructor how to bag the victim instead of using mouth-to-mouth, and Avery found herself looking at his hands again... wondering if they were as capable and rough as they looked.

She swallowed and shoved the thought down. The minute she got out of here, she was going to grab a giant-sized espresso and try to get some kind of focus. She wasn't one to struggle with scattered thoughts or actions, and today of all days, it wasn't welcome.

The instructor gave a nod. "Both of you go to the front, and Shelly will fill out your certification cards. You're free to leave after that, but make sure to grab some snacks before you go."

"Thanks," Jess tossed out, gaining his feet.

Avery pushed to a stand as well and blinked up at Jess. While she was a tall woman, she only reached his shoulders, something quite unusual for her.

The man's a beast.

Turning before she let some stupid words slip out, she led the way to the front. Shelly got their cards to them quickly, and then Avery bypassed the snack table and walked out the door. The hot breeze hit her face. She inhaled deeply.

Jess stepped out beside her. To her surprise, he didn't throw her a wave and a word of goodbye. He hitched a thumb in his front pocket and smiled down at her.

Avery plastered a hand over her face and peeked up at him through her splayed fingers. She groaned. "I'm sorry about that. Today probably wasn't the best day to take the refresher course, but I was signed up for it and didn't want to back out."

He chuckled. "You were fine."

She lowered her hand. "Thank you for saving me on those steps. I just... blanked."

"Been there. Thing is, we don't ever blank when it comes to the real deal."

"That's true." She hesitated. Should she ask him out for coffee? It wasn't any different from having coffee with her partner, right?

He didn't speak for a long moment, and she waited to see if he'd make the first overture. When he didn't, she spoke up.

"I was thinking about a big espresso to wake me up. Would you like to come along with me?"

His brows pinched, and then smoothed just as quickly. "Coffee sounds good."

"There's a little joint down this way. They've got sandwiches too."

"Great—I'm hungry."

She thought a man of his size probably never got filled up and a little sandwich wouldn't do the trick, but having somebody to share lunch with might take her mind off things.

She started down the sidewalk with him at her side. "So what do you do?"

He smiled. "I'm in law enforcement."

Shit—not a cop here in Austin but perhaps a state trooper. She should have known. It also meant he knew about her situation.

"Where are you based?"

"It's a little broader than city law enforcement," he said.

"Oh." She picked up on his don't-ask tone and let it go. Thankfully, the coffee shop was within sight, and she didn't have to say more. When they reached the building with the brown and tan striped awning over the entrance, Jess opened the door for her. She stepped inside to the heavenly scent of freshly ground coffee beans.

As they waited in line to place their orders, Avery tried to think up some mundane conversation that wouldn't put him on edge or herself in the spotlight. She was beginning to regret her rash decision to ask him out.

At her side, he seemed completely at ease, though, his body language relaxed. Maybe she was the one on edge.

When they reached the head of the line, she placed her order of an espresso and chicken salad on a croissant. She started to reach for her purse to pay, when he placed a hand on her arm.

"This is on me," he told the clerk. "I could use a pick-me-up. I'll have an espresso too, and one of those Italian whattayacallits on focaccia bread."

The clerk's smile spread, and Avery felt her own stomach warm in reaction to the man's drawl.

He took out some bills and paid for the meals. As they moved down the line to the pickup area, Avery said, "Thank you. You didn't have to pay."

"Wanted to." His voice was rougher than it had been, leaving her feeling even more out of her comfort zone.

They took their trays and carried them away. The tables were mostly taken, all but one toward the back.

Jess stepped up to one near the windows where they could look out on the street. "Excuse me, were you about to leave? It's a great table for people-watching."

"Actually, yes, we were finished." A man and woman stood and gathered their trash and trays, evacuating the table.

Jess swooped in and snagged it, and Avery sank to the seat across from him. She stared at him. "How did you do that?"

He looked up into her eyes. "Do what?"

"Charm those people into leaving?"

He chuckled. "They were on their way out anyway. I just prompted them along."

She shook her head. The man was a surprise, a refreshing one.

Looking out the window at the pedestrians on the street, she said, "It *is* a great seat for people-watching."

"Yup." He raised his coffee to his lips and moaned around the brew before swallowing. "Mmm. I'll have to remember this place. Best coffee I've had in a long time."

"Yes, I'm not usually in this section of town, but whenever I am, I come here."

He set aside his cup and settled his gaze on her. "Avery…"

Oh no, here it comes.

"I can't start out false with you. I know about the altercation at the grocery store and what you're facing."

She swallowed hard, the espresso she'd wanted so badly minutes before now tasteless on her tongue.

"I was sorry to hear it, and even more sorry now that I know you in person."

"Thank you." She looked up into his stare. The genuine concern in his eyes left her floundering for something else to say.

He nodded. "This is stretching our fledgling friendship, but if you'd allow me, I could maybe see what I can find out for you."

"No, it's okay," she said at once.

He compressed his lips. "I don't mean to overstep. I'm just in the business of helping people."

She tipped her head to the side. "If we're moving along this friendship quickly, then maybe it's already time for me to ask what it is you do. Because you're not a beat cop."

"No." He sipped.

"Investigator?"

"You could say that. Sometimes."

A laugh escaped her. "What does that mean?"

"Sometimes I know how to look for things."

36

She sat back in her chair, staring at him. "Very secretive." Picking up her sandwich, she bit into the flaky croissant and perfect chicken salad.

With a quirk of his lips, he bit into his Italian. "I'm sorry—I don't mean to be secretive. I'm just not allowed to say."

She smiled. "Then don't let me drag it out of you."

* * * * *

Damn, he liked this one.

Which was the problem.

Any of the women he went after ended up unhappy, unsatisfied and out of his life. If he didn't admit he actually enjoyed Avery's company—even to himself—then maybe he could keep talking to her.

Lunch flew by quickly, with the topics ranging all over the place once they started eating. He loved her ideas on offering some CPR classes to middle-schoolers, though he resisted volunteering, which was his urge.

Good food and good company. What more could he ask for today? He also liked the way she tipped her head when in thought.

And he loved watching her lips. Damn, they could stir a man enough to keep him seated for a while.

Yeah, it was best to keep this woman friend-zoned and refrain from asking her out for dinner. Not that his evenings were free. The phone calls between Moreno and his terrorist buddies were now Jess's social life and entertainment.

Too soon their lunch was finished, and they were relinquishing the best table in the coffeeshop to another couple.

"We didn't do much people-watching," she said with a hint of regret as they made their way out of the coffeeshop.

He held back from saying, *Maybe next time.*

On the sidewalk, they faced each other. "I'm parked back by the station," he said.

"So am I."

Good—they could walk together and this strangely comfortable moment didn't need to come to an end quite yet.

After several letdowns and past women troubles, he'd withdrawn himself more and more. Rejection was damn hard to swallow, and the thought of getting the same old excuses from Avery wasn't something he was up for today, or any day, for that matter.

He kept the talk light as they returned to their vehicles. As he walked beside her to an economy car, she placed a hand on his arm.

A jolt of heat clawed through muscle and flesh.

He stared into her eyes. How easy it would be to fall into those brown depths and see what really made Avery tick. And hear more about her true feelings on the event that had gotten her suspended.

"Thanks again for lunch and for saving me at the class," she said. Though she moved her hand away, her touch remained, a warm brand on his skin. He half expected to see a print on his flesh where her fingers had rested for so brief a moment.

"My pleasure. I wish you the best on your review, Avery."

She pressed her lips together and released them, making him look harder at the perfect shape of her mouth.

"Thank you." She looked up at him as if wanting to say more. In the end, she turned for her car door, and he glimpsed some towels covering her seat. Suddenly, she swung back to him. "Why don't you give me your phone number? Then next time I'm near the coffeeshop, I'll give you a call."

Surprise hit him. But on the heels of that was a hefty dose of depression. She'd never call. Or if she did, she'd finally confide she had a fiancé, was making honeymoon plans in the Bahamas. Or giving him one of many other lines he'd heard over the years with chicks.

To think men got a bad rep for being noncommittal. He knew way more women who weren't interested in more than a one-night stand.

Or maybe it was just him.

"I'd like that," he said, instead of all the crap running through his mind. He recited his number, and she climbed into her car. He gave her a wave and smile.

As he walked back to his old Mustang that his brother had helped him rebuild, Jess scuffed his boot at a loose part of the asphalt.

Well… I'll never hear from that one again.

Chapter Three

"Jess, can I talk to you?"

He pivoted from his locker to see his captain Nash Sullivan standing there. The grim-as-fuck look on his face didn't bode well.

"Yeah, let me get outta this gear," he said to Sully. As his commander went off toward the office, Jess first removed all the weapons he carried—rifle, sidearm, knife. Following that, he stowed away everything from Kevlar vest to boots and then dressed in his civvies of jeans, T-shirt and old boots.

He'd rub a hand over his face, but it would get the cut on his brow bleeding again, and he'd just gotten it to stop. The ride across the state had been a hell of a long one, and each and every Ranger Ops man was feeling the aftereffects of what they'd been through.

So many fucking radical militia types out there for anybody's peace of mind. Texas was full o' them. It took all of ten seconds for one of the asshole's fuses to ignite and then the entire fucking country was at risk. What the common population didn't know...

Lennon caught him by the shoulder. "Hey, Jess, good shot you made out there. Saved my ass. Thank you."

He gave a hard nod. "Wasn't in the mood to carry your heavy ass outta there, Reed."

Lennon shot him a crooked smile and went about stashing his own gear in his locker. "See ya at the bowling alley tomorrow."

Their hangout. It'd been a long time since Jess had joined the guys there, had a few games over beers.

"Sure." If he wasn't listening to Moreno tomorrow night.

He headed toward the office. Sully wasn't seated at the desk. In fact, Jess had never seen his captain seated there, not being the desk-jockey type.

He turned from the window, where he was staring through the small chinks of light permeating the cracks in the blinds. Which really meant Sully had been staring at nothing at all.

Jess's guts tensed. "What's up?" he asked.

Sully eyed him. "Got some intel on Moreno."

He and Jess were the only two people in Ranger Ops who knew what was going down, and the reason was the rest wouldn't need to be briefed on it until the day they went after the spy.

Jess folded his arms and waited for it.

"Edgar Ortiz is dead."

42

The statement had Jess wide-eyed and staring at Sully. "What the fuck happened?"

"This happened." He opened a file on his desk and tossed an eight-by-ten photo across the surface at Jess.

He scooped it up. His gut clenched at the sight of the twisted remains of Ortiz. Friend of Moreno.

He jerked his gaze up. "Who?" he grated out.

"Homeland says Fernandez."

"Jesus Christ. Ortiz was this Fernandez's friend. Night before last, he just told Moreno he and Fernandez were going to a soccer game next week."

"Well, guess the new plan was to off his best friend."

"Fuck. I can't believe it. When?"

"News came in this morning. I just had a moment to finally examine it."

Jess glanced down at the photo and then away. "Time of death?"

"They're saying ten a.m. on Monday."

"Fuck that. I don't buy that it was by Fernandez's own hand, not at that time of day."

Sully folded his arms. "Why not?"

"The guy..." His mind reeled, thoughts out of order. "Moreno just attended religious services with Fernandez and his children, an early mass for some saint or other. He wasn't anywhere near Ortiz."

43

"Some people are good at keeping public appearances. Inside, they're monsters. Besides, doesn't mean Fernandez didn't call out a hit on the guy. Or that Moreno wasn't somehow involved."

Jess shook his head. "I don't know about that. Moreno sells intelligence—he doesn't order hits. And Moreno and Ortiz were chummy on phone calls. Nothing off at all. Do you think he took his kid to church, prayed with him, and meanwhile he was blowing up his friend?"

"Maybe they weren't that close of friends," Sully said wryly.

Jess's brows shot up.

"It's a bad joke. I'm just tryin' to lighten the mood. You okay, man? You've been burning the candles at both ends for weeks. I'll tell the other analyst to look into this shit with Ortiz. You should go home and get some rest."

"I'm fine." His voice was gritty. He chalked it up to needing sleep, but Sully looked at him with those eagle-sharp eyes.

Jess scrubbed a hand through his hair. "Am I fucking missing something in these conversations? Tell me. You've heard them."

"Yeah, I have, and no, you're not. I think most things can't be spoken over the phone, and that's where we're lacking. We can only move on what we learn from listening or texts we intercept."

"Why the hell don't we have somebody in there undercover?" Jess passed a hand over his face and felt the cut on his brow break open again. Warm blood started to trickle down his cheek.

Sully glanced at him and tossed him a box of tissues from his desk. Jess took a few with a jerk of his hand and pressed them to his face.

"All I can say is we're doing our part. You're getting lots of good intel for OFFSUS, and you need to keep up the good work."

"Bullshit," he responded. "They've got me on the losing end of a battle, and the shit I hear isn't enough to give us information on the next attack that kills a hundred people." All Jess heard on these calls was that Moreno was a decent father and friend. He loved soccer, his kids…

And maybe helping to blow up his friends.

"Keep on it, Jess. But don't be afraid to speak up when you need a break from it. You can't get too close."

He pushed out a breath. "Hazard of the job. I'm fine. Thanks for informing me about Ortiz's death. I'll see what I can find out."

"Get some stitches in that cut."

He removed the tissue wad from it. "I've got medical super-glue at home that'll take care of it. See ya later, Sully."

The entire drive home, Jess replayed the conversation with his commander as well as the intel.

Ortiz killed while Fernandez and Moreno, his friends, sat in church? They were no saints themselves, and it *would* be a good alibi if pressed for one.

It raised more questions on Moreno too. Was it fucking possible the man was colder than Jess thought him to be? So duplicitous that he would have given warm wishes to his friend just hours before he assisted Fernandez in leaving Ortiz mangled, his face nearly unrecognizable?

There was little Jess could have done.

He grunted. Sure, he told himself that, but did he buy it?

He went into his condo and threw more dirty clothes onto the pile in his bedroom. Bare-ass naked, he walked into the bathroom and turned the shower as hot as it would go. His ribs still ached, and the new cut stung like a bitch when it got wet, but he let the water flow over it for long minutes to clean out the worst.

When he stepped from the shower and dried off, he saw a text flash up on his phone. He groaned. It better not be Sully again. He'd never admit it to the man, but he needed a damn break.

He plucked his phone off the sink and read the message, heart launching upward before sinking again.

The bungee cord effect he'd come to expect from any interaction with a woman he enjoyed being around.

It was a text from Avery.

Do you have time to meet and talk? I could use an ear.

Shit. What was even happening with her review? He hadn't heard a peep about it, and he'd respected her wishes and hadn't gone digging for information.

He thumbed his reply. *Name the place and time and I'll be there.*

He hoped that didn't sound overly eager. And fuck it if it did. He was finished trying to think ahead about what women wanted. Avery was just a friend asking for someone to listen to her.

So far, she wasn't like the other women he'd been with—who liked the way he looked and asked for the dangerous sex to match his muscles, and then they left when he finally let them close enough to learn that danger was his life.

Avery wasn't asking for anything more than probably coffee and a discussion about her internal review.

She replied with a time and place, and he grabbed a clean shirt off the top of his dresser. Part of him wondered if he should clean up his bedroom, change the sheets and do his laundry in the event he did get lucky enough to bring Avery home.

The other part said *fat chance* and ignored it. He finished dressing, ran his fingers through his wet hair and managed to get his cut bleeding again.

Damn, he'd forgotten about the glue. He went back to the bathroom and dug the first-aid kit from under the sink. A couple minutes later, he was patched up and ready to rumble once more.

His libido had thoughts of a roll in the sack with the beautiful and tough Avery Aarons. But that wasn't going to happen. Most he could hope for was that she'd be wearing those sexy yoga pants again.

* * * * *

Avery rested her hands on the tabletop to keep from clenching them into fists. Outside the coffeeshop window, street traffic was at its peak of the day as people went about their normal activities. Work, lunch break, work, then home to their families.

Avery didn't have any of that. Right now, she only had her fury and a tall latte before her and Jess staring at her with the same expression she wore.

She was pissed, and the fact he was on her behalf just let her know she really wasn't losing her mind.

"So you think all this is a shit show too?" she asked again.

He nodded. "You're being investigated for discharging a firearm on a man who reached for his waistband — and what you believed was a weapon. It should be cut and dry, since the guy also has a history of weapons charges. Why are they digging into your past now?"

She pushed out a breath. "There's more." She'd shared the campus attack with Jess, because the board had thrown it in her face this morning, saying she needed a deeper psych eval as part of the investigation. As if she hadn't already had dozens before becoming a cop. She'd checked out in all those.

Jess's gaze remained fixed on her face, his own battered and worn with fatigue. What the hell had he been doing to get that deep cut on his brow?

"I'm listening," he said.

She twisted her fingers together. "When I was ten, some guys broke into the house. I was alone, my parents out for the evening with friends."

"Jesus, Avery."

She swallowed against the emotion those two little words of sympathy and outrage raised inside her. "I'm over it, of course. I had counseling afterward and moved on. But I feel as if the board is trying to say I'm seeking revenge on all men because I've experienced two personal crimes in my lifetime. Actually, one of the guys suggested that I really saw that guy in the parking lot as the same one who broke in and terrified me as a child."

Jess leaned in, eyes flashing. "That's what he said to you?"

She nodded. "Somebody did some deep digging to unearth that little tidbit from my past."

"Fuckers," he said under his breath.

She nodded. "I'm sorry to throw this all at you. It's my problem, not yours."

"Avery, there are things I can access... look into for you."

49

What exactly did Jess do for a living that he'd have access to classified files?

She bit her lip, wondering if letting him investigate would help her in any way or just get her badge melted down into scrap metal.

"Say the word, and I'll make a call," he said.

"Thank you. I'll think on it."

He gave a single nod, the masculine move shifting her attention away from herself and the mess she was in. "Are you okay? What happened to your face?"

He lifted a shoulder and let it fall. "Ran into a rifle butt."

"Hell." Okay, really, what did he do for a living?

Sipping his coffee, he just looked at her. The man was all secrets while she was an open book. She was embarrassed by her blabbering.

"I'm fine. Listen, Avery, do you have someone on your side during this review process? A neutral party who can fight for you?"

"Yes. Plus there's evidence from the security camera footage as well as a witness who was coming out of the store when I pulled the trigger. He gave a statement that he believed the man to be reaching for a weapon as well."

Jess set down his cup and rested a hand on the back of her knotted ones. The touch was so brief, a skimming of warm, rough flesh over hers. Her gaze flew to his.

She opened her mouth to thank him for being a friend when she needed it most, but suddenly a young girl stepped up to the table. She was dressed like any youth, in jeans and a graphic T-shirt with a flannel tied around her hips. She looked nervous, though, chewing at her lip.

Jess looked up and something passed over his features, wrecking the neutral façade Avery was used to seeing. Then it was back in place just as quickly as it had fled.

"Uh, Jess?" the girl said.

He gave a forceful clearing of his throat. "Hi."

Was it Avery's imagination, or was that single word heated with emotion?

"I thought that was you."

"Are you here with your mom?" He turned in his chair to face the girl.

She nodded. "I had a doctor's appointment, so we ate lunch before she takes me back to school."

He nodded. Nothing special, just a nod. But Avery could swear the tension in his muscles was building underneath that army-green T-shirt he wore.

"I hope you're not sick?" he asked.

"It was just a checkup." She looked even more nervous. "Um, I have something I wanted to ask you. I have to do a project on a family tree. I was hoping you could help me." She darted a glance at Avery for the first time.

Avery gave her a gentle smile in return.

51

She flicked her attention back to Jess, who'd inched to the edge of his seat as if ready to spring up. "Will you help me?" she asked.

"Of course I will, sweetheart. A family tree. I can do that. I'll… get with your mother about giving you the information. Does that sound okay?"

She nodded. "Thanks, Jess."

He swallowed hard. "I'm happy to help."

Avery watched the young girl move back across the coffeeshop to a woman who must be her mother. They shared the same warm brown hair color.

Jess was still, gripping the edge of the table as he watched her walk away. His knuckles whitened.

"Jess, are you all right?" Avery asked in a quiet tone.

He swung his stare up to hers, and it took a second for his eyes to clear with recognition.

"You seem far away," she noted.

"Yeah."

"A family tree project. Is that your niece?"

"No." His green-and-gold eyes closed off as a mist clouded them. He dropped his stare to the table and his fingertips dug into the wood. "No," he said again in a thick voice. "She's my daughter."

* * * * *

Jesus Christ. She was so grown up.

And he'd just been sucker-punched in the goddamn gut.

Avery was still and quiet, watching him while trying to appear not to stare. His food suddenly went from something gourmet to rotten slime on his plate, and when he raised his coffee to his lips, it had gone cold.

What the hell did he even say now? How did a man who hadn't seen his daughter since she was ten act normal?

When Avery reached across the table and placed a hand over his, he looked up into her eyes.

"I'm sorry for my behavior. I think I'm going to cut our lunch short."

She nodded and stood when he did. She dumped her half-eaten food in the trash the same as him and followed him outside, still clinging to her paper coffee cup.

They walked for a bit, and he didn't see anything except his kid's eyes, the same damn color as his own. It might be the only fucking link to her he had.

Except now she wanted help—with a family tree project. Only he had about as much knowledge of his family as she did, namely his father's side.

Next to him, Avery walked along, silent and unexpecting. It wasn't a quiet that made him feel he had to ramble on or tell his story. It was just... comfortable.

He turned to her suddenly and let out a humorless chuckle. "You must think I'm crazy."

Her brows rose, the perfect arches drawing more attention to how beautiful her eyes were. "And here I thought you must think I'm crazy, telling you about my past traumas and how they could result in me never getting back my badge. At least I didn't tell you that I've always felt fate is coming for me, that I'll die by some violent crime." She clapped a mocking hand over her mouth. "Well, there it was."

He gave a rueful chuckle. Rubbing his fingers against his sore jaw, he said, "We make quite a pair."

"Look, Jess, you've got my number."

"You've got mine." He slowed his pace as they reached where his truck was parked.

"Oh great — you've got a parking ticket."

He saw the envelope tucked under his wiper blade. He removed it and tossed it into his truck. It landed on the floor of the passenger's side with about thirty others.

Avery peeked in and saw this. A bemused smile crossed her face. "You looking to get arrested for not paying parking tickets?"

"I'm not worried about it."

"I see."

"No, you don't. You can't, because I haven't been straightforward with you. Look, I'm going to go home and take care of some shit. Next time we get together, maybe I'll tell you my life story too."

Her smile softened. When she turned her almond-shaped eyes up at him like that, he had the overwhelming urge to lean in, cup her face and kiss her. His insides clutched at the thought.

"Deal. Next time, we'll make it dinner."

"You're on." He shot her what smile he could muster before grabbing her hand and giving it a squeeze. "Later, then."

"Later," she echoed in his same tone, which gave him a chuckle before he got into his truck. When he pulled away from the curb, he glanced back to see Avery continuing on, walking to her own vehicle. Part of him felt bad for not seeing her safe to her car, but she could handle herself if a situation arose.

His brain settled on his daughter. Madison was fourteen now, a true beauty like her mother, who had turned his head back when he was young, dumb and full of cum. But fact was, the moment he'd learned about the baby, he'd asked Jenna to marry him. Of course, her answer had been no, and ten seconds after that, she'd dumped him.

That fateful day had kicked off a series of explosions surrounding each and every one of his relationships. The curse had begun there, but the true curse, he'd come to realize more and more as years passed, was not knowing his own child.

Now her hair was so long, her body filling out into those curves that a dad should get out a shotgun to defend.

And she'd called him Jess—not Dad.

His stomach cramped with the pain of that. God, he should have fought Jenna for partial custody. But fact was, his shift work over the years would have made shared custody damn difficult to plan. And a kid needed routines, which he wasn't able to offer.

In the end, he'd agreed to stay out of Madison's life so as not to confuse her, but she knew who he was, recognized him enough to pick him out in a crowded coffeeshop.

A seed of hope bloomed in his core. Maybe, just maybe, this project was a cracked door between them. He could use the opportunity to close that door or fling it wide.

She was older now, would understand why her father wasn't around as much because of his work. He could take time for her between missions.

Throat tight with emotion, he mentally listed the people he knew off the top of his head on his branch of the family tree. His momma, maternal grandparents, brothers and their wives and children. An aunt who lived in Rehoboth Beach and her husband who was a lifer in the Air Force.

By the time he reached home, he was ready to dig into the ancestry research, but instead he came up against a brick wall when Colonel Downs ordered him to tune in and listen to the latest phone conversation between Moreno and a man he likely shouldn't be speaking with—if he wanted his kids to have their father.

* * * * *

"Let's go! And one… two… three… jab… four!"

The kickboxing class instructor shouted the moves, but Avery barely heard them. Her body was a machine, moving automatically with all the energy and fight she had, even as her mind wandered.

Okay, wandered didn't exactly describe it—her brain was a hitchhiking hippie free-bird. Roaming from one topic to the next, she'd touched on the internal review and what the board might be digging up about her right this minute, to the officer who'd replaced her and how he and Reggie were getting along. Reggie didn't welcome a lot of chatter while on duty. He liked to concentrate. And since Avery wasn't someone to just speak for the sake of hearing herself, they got along fine.

Then her doomsday way of thinking would kick in and she'd wonder what job she could do if they really did take her badge forever. She couldn't picture herself as anything but a cop.

After that, she contemplated moving out of state, but she was a Texas girl at heart.

Which brought her back around to the question of why she felt connected to a state where she had no family. Her mother and father had moved to the Florida Keys, and she had no siblings or even a boyfriend to hold her here. Hell, all her friends were in the force and if she was kicked out, she wasn't likely to be invited to holiday parties or backyard barbecues.

She jabbed to the right and to the left. The uppercut felt damn good, the roundhouse kick better. Her muscles burned, and after another half hour, cramped. Sweat rolled off her, and that increased as thoughts of Jess pooled in her mind.

The look on his face when he'd seen his daughter... God, Avery had seen big men tear up before, cops at funerals for their fallen brothers, but somehow on Jess, it had only made her interest in him grow.

She'd gone from being attracted to the man and thankful for his friendship to wanting... more... all in the scope of five seconds.

He didn't seem to be interested in her that way, though. He'd never made a move on her and didn't send her flirty texts despite him having her number. Perhaps he was still involved with the child's mother or hadn't gotten over her.

Funny how Avery felt she knew Jess in many ways but at the same time knew nothing at all.

Fact was... if Jess came anywhere near her apartment, she'd ask him to come in. And spend the night. And share breakfast.

Maybe she just needed to kickbox harder, work out some of these sexual tensions she had pent-up for a man who probably didn't return the sentiment.

She could swear she'd caught him staring at her mouth more than once, though. At the time, it had been during lunch, so it could be he thought she chewed weird or had lettuce in her teeth.

The instructor turned down the intensity dial, and they moved into a cool-down phase. Avery felt as if she could go on for another hour at least. Her early days with the ROTC had provided her with stamina, and since she had nothing better to do with her time, she had a water break and then hit the gym's track.

Her run started as determined, but soon became a leisurely jog, allowing her time to reflect more on her situation. Thing was, on top of the internal review, she still had to deal with the ramifications of shooting a man.

That was stuff that sent big, brawny cops to therapy. She'd seen it before. Maybe it was time for her to talk to someone as well, find a shrink on her own and not one ordered by the board.

The decision helped her find a sense of calm for the day, which she had been hoping for by physically exhausting herself. Funny how the mind and body and spirit were rarely one. Typically, her body was a screaming drill sergeant while her mind overthought things and her spirit told her to just have some caffeine and brush it off.

Damn, she *was* a mess.

After hitting the showers, she left the gym, her hand going to her phone. But once she looked at the screen, she thought twice about texting Jess as she'd originally planned.

Last thing she wanted to do was crowd him. A man like that wouldn't invite such clinginess into his life—she'd only drive him away, and she didn't want that.

She liked him.

A lot.

Everything was more confusing when added to the rest of her messy life. But she hadn't enjoyed the company of a man like Jess in forever. If she was honest, she hadn't allowed herself to get close since the attack back in college. It was hard to trust anybody after that.

Jess was different.

He also was totally uninterested in her. He'd only had coffee to be nice and provide a listening ear.

Ugh—if she had a girlfriend, she could run all this by her, but all her friends were guys. Reggie would just laugh and tell her to go for it, but that wouldn't exactly be helpful.

Now she was right back where she'd started, her body telling her to work off some steam, that she wasn't nearly tired enough yet.

Maybe once she got home she'd take a walk around the park and try to clear her mind again. Problem was, if she didn't deal with everything, in time she'd run out of places to escape.

Chapter Four

Jess dressed in silence, but around him the Ranger Ops team were bullshitting about their kids and significant others. Down the line of lockers, Cav's voice reached Jess as he reported on his latest conquest.

Lennon laughed at what he was saying and asked if she was jailbait. Cav chuckled in return and told him she was twenty-six. Lennon gave a nod. "Much better," he said.

"Well, she's got more experience in bed," Cav responded.

Jess turned his face toward his locker, but it was mostly empty, all his gear strapped onto his body.

He closed the door and turned to walk away.

Sully was already finished and waiting for them all to load into the SUV and hit the road for parts unknown. The briefing would come during the trip.

Whatever the threat, Jess wasn't afraid of staring it in the eyes.

But he was terrified of messing up with his daughter.

He'd lain awake for three nights thinking about it. Somewhere before dawn that first day, he'd risen from his twisted sheets and subscribed to an ancestry website to help with his research. That was as far as he'd gotten, because the past few solid days had been spent on Moreno.

When he finally got a free moment, he hadn't even typed in his father's name before he'd gotten the call to arms from Sully.

As he approached his leader, Sully grabbed his shoulder. "You all right?"

"Yep."

He looked at him hard. "This about Moreno?"

"No. Though now that's weighing on my mind too, thanks."

Sully released his shoulder. "If you're not up for this—"

"I am. Just let me do my job, okay?"

Sully compressed his lips and gave a nod. He let him pass, and Jess walked out of the building. He climbed into his usual spot in the very back of the vehicle and waited for the others.

Cav got in first. He shot Jess a look before landing heavily in the seat next to his. "You good, man?"

"The fucking best."

"You sound it. What's going on? More women troubles?"

"Could say that." His daughter was practically a woman, right?

But now that Cav had suggested it, a perfect image of Avery floated across Jess's mind.

The woman was everything he would have gone for months ago, but he was too gun-shy to make a move. Besides, she didn't need more complications in her life, not with what she had going on.

Cav asked him another question, which he answered in a monosyllable. Taking the hint he wasn't feeling very talkative, Cav joined into Lennon and Linc's conversation instead.

When they hit the highway headed south, they all groaned, except Jess who didn't give a fuck where they were going, let alone back to Mexico.

"Man, we've spent so much time in Coahuila that I feel I should be a resident there by now," Woody griped from the passenger's seat.

"Dual citizenship at least, right?" Sully responded, stepping on the gas and overtaking the produce truck ahead of them.

Jess barely listened to their talk. His mind skipped over his own issues, mainly how to get into his daughter's life. Was it too late to have that relationship with her? God, he didn't know.

He had a hell of a lot of guilt about his own failures with Madison. That started him thinking about another father... Moreno. They were no closer to finding Ortiz's killer, but all that seemed dimmed by the fact Moreno had done exactly what they'd expected from him—he'd delivered sensitive information into the hands of a radical group known for two bombings of major cities.

Moreno's hours were numbered.

His time with his children numbered.

"That woman who shot the guy in the supermarket parking lot." Cav's statement had Jess's head snapping up.

"Yeah, tough break for her. Makes me glad I'm not walkin' the beat again," Lennon said.

"Thing is, if she'd walked away from that scene and not gotten involved, she would have been crucified for it if anybody had found out she was there. Not to mention not being able to live with herself if something worse had happened to the woman involved in the domestic." This from Linc.

Jess clenched a fist on his knee and listened without adding anything of his own. The guys all agreed Avery should be supported for it and the internal review shouldn't have taken more than thirty seconds to deliberate—Avery had stopped one more abuser, and the fewer the better, in the Ranger Ops' opinion.

With Avery in his mind now, Jess had to seriously think about what he wanted out of a friendship with her. Great coffee, amazing conversation?

Hell, who was he kidding? He wanted to bend her over the table by the window and fuck her right there for everyone to see.

Jesus, that was a little stronger reaction than normal, even for a guy like him.

And he was known for getting in deep quick.

Bottom line—he couldn't trust his feelings about Avery. She was beautiful and available, but that didn't mean she wanted more with him, and he couldn't risk complicating her life more than it already was. He kept telling himself that, but he wasn't really listening.

The rest of the drive went by with more talk he did not join into. Nobody asked him anything, and he was grateful to be overlooked. When they arrived at their destination, Cav blew out a breath.

"Jesus, even the air stinks here," he said.

Jess grunted.

Cav glanced at him. "You good, dude?"

"The best. Let's get this shit over with."

Sully's instructions during the ride replayed in Jess's mind. They were facing a couple of weapons dealers who'd recently dabbled in some darker shit when they traded weapons for women. One of these women had been sold to an undercover, and the entire operation had been broken open like an oozing, filthy wound.

The minute the undercover agent had leaked their position to the government and the Ranger Ops had been called in, the undercover had been executed. They were down here to not only stop these guys but to recover their own agent's body and take it home for a proper burial.

The mission wasn't as dark as they sometimes dealt with, but it added to Jess's mood. He remained silent, focused.

After they got into position, Cav nudged him. "You're worryin' me, man. You never stay this quiet for this long."

"I'm fine. Just got some things on my mind."

At that moment, Sully's order came, and there was no more time to talk. He and Cav rushed the door. He shot the lock off while Cav kicked it in. Jess ran inside first, swinging left and right, searching the building for threats.

Cav's heavy footfalls sounded behind Jess. There was a sudden shout as their presence was discovered, and Jess turned his adrenaline into action.

He whipped around a corner, took aim and fired. The man fell, howling in pain, the leg Jess had shot out from under him twisted to the side. Before he could reach for a weapon, Jess was on him, Cav as backup.

"Tie him up," Jess said roughly.

The man cussed at him, and Jess pressed a boot down on his broken leg. As the guy's eyes rolled up in his head and he passed out, Jess spun away, watching for other threats. Shouts volleyed throughout the building. Another shot rang out.

Cav got the unconscious man bound and gagged. They wanted this one alive, because he was one of the ringleaders, and any information they got out of him was needed to locate the rest of the group.

Cav hoisted the man up and over his shoulder as if he weighed a hundred pounds instead of two hundred. They started out of the room, when Jess caught a sound.

He did another sweep of the room, but it was empty, just as he'd first thought.

"There a closet somewhere around here?" he ground out to Cav.

The man over his shoulder came to and barfed. The sick fluid splashed down Cav's back and hit the floor.

"Jesus Christ. Why do I always get the pukers?" Cav tossed the man to the floor, and he groaned.

Jess turned his head to listen harder. There, under the rhythm of his own heart, was a faint cry.

"Fucking hell." He strode to the wall and put his ear to it. A small thump sounded again. He met Cav's stare. "There's a door. Check the other room."

A minute later, Cav was back, shaking his head. "No doors."

"You don't think… Fuck. They're hiding them in the walls."

Into his comms unit, he said, "Do not shoot into any of the walls. They've got some hidden there!"

The knocking that followed had the hair on the back of Jess's neck standing on end. Cav was screaming at the man on the floor, demanding he tell Cav everything he knew, while Jess started circling the room, a hand on the wall to feel for a cutout panel or any way of getting inside.

The pounding sound was weak. He followed it, ear pressed to the plaster. When he turned to look at Cav, he found horror on his buddy's face.

"Fuck. Get her outta there, Jess."

He gave a nod and smashed his rifle butt into the wall several feet above where he'd heard the sound.

The space between walls was thick, or at least this one was. His rifle sank deep. Plaster crumbled at his feet.

When a muffled cry sounded, he tried to see inside the hole he'd made. It was dark, so he shined his light in and nearly had a fucking heart attack at the sight of three pairs of eyes.

"Two women and a child here. Help me, Cav."

They started bashing apart the wall using their rifles and gloved hands to tear away the plaster. When the hole was large enough for a woman to squeeze through, he reached inside to take her by the hands. She slipped out onto the floor—dirty, half-starved, blinking at the light.

"Holy fuck," Sully said from the doorway. He stormed up to the man who was tied and ripped the gag down to his chin. "How many fucking more are there?" he screamed into his face.

The man glared defiantly at their captain, and Sully wasn't standing for it. He pointed his rifle at the man's uninjured leg. "Tell me or I'll give you a matching bullet hole!"

When silence was the only answer, the shot rang out. Roars of pain sounded, along with a number in Spanish that had Jess's gut clenching and Sully giving the order to open up every single fucking wall in the place.

The other two women were pulled free, and it turned out the child was an adolescent boy. All three were dressed in rags.

Jess gave them his water bottle. "Can you speak?" He squatted before one.

She nodded and took a sip.

"How did you get in the wall? Where is the door?" he asked fluently in her language.

She pointed downward.

He swung his gaze to Sully's. "Under the building."

"We're on it. Woody, you're with me," Sully called out, and a second later Woody met him outside the door of the room.

The women threw her writhing captor on the floor terrified glances. Jess moved to block him from

69

their view. "He can't hurt you anymore. Where are you from?"

After some prodding, he learned they were taken out of their cousin's home and brought here in exchange for a case of guns. They had been kept in a holding space beneath the house, where it was all dirt floor and had bugs and vermin. They were told to move upward into the spaces between walls at certain times a day or when they heard visitors come. Inside the walls were small ledges where they could rest and get footing.

"They're told to wait in hiding in case anybody raided this place," Jess said, getting up from his crouch. He reached into his pack and came out with two MRE rations. He handed them to the trio and they tore into the food to share.

He approached Cav, who still stood guard over the man on the floor.

Jess glared at him. "I'd love to blow his balls off."

Cav gave a resigned nod. "Fucking deserves it if we peel them each like an egg then cut them off and feed them to the rats."

Acknowledgement slid into the man's eyes. He understood what they said.

"Sixteen. We've got sixteen coming out," Woody's voice projected into their comms units.

Jess began to interrogate their hostage. Each question more demanding than the last. When the man failed to answer quick enough, Jess threatened to feed his balls to the rats like Cav suggested.

Finally, Lennon came into the room. He threw Jess a look and then exchanged one with Cav before walking over to the trio they'd rescued and leading them outside. When Linc entered, he walked up to Jess and gripped his shoulder.

"We're takin' him alive. You can stand down," Linc said.

Jess's jaw hurt from grinding his teeth. He spat at the man. "Not yet. I think he deserves to be just as frightened as the people he's kept captive, don't you, Linc?"

Linc's grip tightened on his shoulder, his fingers digging into the tendons. "Go outside and leave this to me and Cav."

Jess stood there a moment, rigid. Then he stalked out of the room on what felt like wooden legs. He continued through the front door and past the people huddled in the yard. Two more men were tied up and gagged, held at gunpoint by Woody.

Sully watched Jess continue by without stopping him.

He had no fucking idea how to feel about any of this. As Ranger Ops, he saw a hell of a lot of stuff. Shit worse than this. But for some reason, right now, he couldn't deal with it. He wanted to slit the throats of the men responsible and watch them bleed out like the pigs they were.

Cav was at his side. "Jess."

He whirled on his friend. "Back off."

Cav's brows shot up. "I'm not the enemy, man. You haven't been yourself all day. What the hell's going on?"

"What's going on is there are too many goddamn evil people in this world."

And he couldn't protect anybody he cared about from them. His daughter… even Avery. She was dealing with her own evil, had been suspended, restricted from stopping more of the same.

"We do that every single day, Jess. One at a time. We can't save the world, but we do our parts."

Cav's words penetrated through his haze of anger.

"Now," Cav drawled out, "tell me what the fuck's really wrong, because I'm not letting it go till you do."

Jess's shoulders slumped. He rubbed a hand over his face. "Guess it's a lot of late nights recently."

Cav eyed him. There was a reason he was known as the weapon of mass destruction on the Ranger Ops team—one glare could send a man into his grave. But Jess was far from intimidated.

"The phone calls?" Cav asked.

Jess's gaze shot to his buddy's. "How do you know about it?"

"We all fucking know. Each one of us is deep in each other's business. It's how we watch each other's

72

backs, remember? Now is that really the issue, because I sense it's more."

"That's it," he lied, not wishing to get into the other things weighing on his mind. For one, none of the guys knew he even had a daughter let alone a teenaged one. And Avery was a whole other reason for them to get in his business, and he wasn't up for that.

Yeah, he wasn't himself. But he intended to fix that — as soon as he was back on US soil.

* * * * *

Avery had attended nine classes at the gym in six days, and she'd run about twenty miles, by her estimate. Her body could handle it, but her mind was another story. If she didn't find a new place to channel her energy, she'd go crazy waiting on this review board to come to a conclusion.

It also didn't help that the only person she wanted to talk to hadn't answered her texts.

She'd left Jess three in total, one asking him to dinner. When dinnertime came and went, she tried another tack, foregoing a meal and suggesting he meet her in the park for a run. After that, she'd felt pretty embarrassed and only sent him a silly meme of a dog waving.

She hitched the strap of her gym bag higher on her shoulder and reached for the door handle just as her phone vibrated with an incoming text. She stopped on the sidewalk and pulled out her phone.

As soon as she spotted Jess's name, her heart gave a very hard, very telling squeeze. *Okay, that was more than an I-like-you squeeze.*

When she glanced at the text, her heart jolted again.

I'm so sorry I didn't reply to you. I was away, but I'm a rotten friend for not explaining why. Can I see you soon?

A smile spread over her face, the first real smile since the shooting.

She quickly thumbed a response. *Yes, I'm about to hit the gym but I already worked out today. I can skip leg afternoon.*

Haha. I've got a few things to do here. Then I need to start on that family tree.

Her thumbs poised over the screen. She could insinuate herself into his day... or walk into the gym and hit the weight room again.

If you'd like some help with the research, I'm up for it.

She held her breath. Somebody stepped up to the door beside her. "Excuse me," he said.

She apologized and moved away from the entrance she was blocking. Heart thrumming faster, she waited for Jess's reply.

If he didn't want help, she wasn't out anything, she tried to remind herself. She was probably depending on him to keep her mind off things more than she should anyway.

The text popped up.

Give me an hour to clean up. An address followed.

Avery flicked her gaze up to the sign hanging over the entrance. She wasn't going to work out yet again and get sweaty before going over to Jess's place. In fact, maybe she should go home and change out of her spandex pants and tank top.

As she turned to head back to her apartment, she found herself smiling intermittently. Each time she caught herself doing it, she felt a small pang of guilt. Should she be happy at all after the error she'd made in the grocery store parking lot that night? After all, the man she'd shot was still in the hospital, having undergone a surgery to repair the damage her bullet had done. He sure wasn't smiling.

But it was part of the job—she had protected that woman and maybe a bystander who might have tried to jump in and stop him from hurting his girlfriend. She was so lost in her thoughts she didn't see the squad car pull up to the curb beside her until she heard the whoop of the siren.

She spun to see Reggie's smiling face. He rolled down the passenger's side window, and Avery stepped up to the car.

"Reg, it's good to see you."

"You too, Ave. Comin' from the gym?" He noted her hair in the ponytail and her attire.

Rather than try to explain, she nodded. "Been there a lot lately. You don't realize how boring being off is until you're forced to be."

"You should come by my house this weekend. Delilah's been asking about you. I'll throw some burgers on the grill." He grinned.

Avery nodded. "I'd like that, thanks. You doin' all right? Where's your sidekick?"

"Reassigned. I'm solo street patrol only for now."

"Oh man, I didn't mean to screw up your job too."

"It's okay—I don't mind just cruisin' around looking for speeders or people running red lights." He gave her a serious look. "You heard about that guy's girlfriend, didn't you?"

Avery blinked. Her mind hadn't caught up to his words. "What do you mean?"

"She was pregnant that night he was roughing her up. I guess before you arrived on the scene, he'd punched her in the stomach a couple times, and she lost the baby."

"Jesus." She dropped her face into her palm.

"You shouldn't feel bad about takin' some scum like that off the street, Ave. I'd have done the same damn thing. Only I wouldn't have just nicked his heart—I would have exploded it."

"Well, now I feel like you're just bragging." She didn't know how to feel about what Reggie had just told her. In the end, she went with what she knew about humanity—many times you couldn't explain their actions. You just tried to keep them all safe.

Feeling worn out from the conversation, she gave Reggie a nod. "Get on with ya. Call me with a time for those burgers."

"I will. Delilah will be happy to see you. Take care of yourself, honey."

"You too." She threw him a wink, and he pulled away from the curb.

All the way back to her apartment, Avery's mind lingered over all he'd said. Then she realized something very important—she'd been filling her time with workouts to try to distract herself. Fact was, she might not welcome the time away from her duties, but she needed it to process what she'd done, to get her head on straight.

She changed into jeans and a decent top in case she and Jess went out for a bite to eat later. After pulling her hair from the elastic band, she ran a brush through it, letting it fall around her shoulders in waves. Then on second thought, she added a dash of berry lipstick.

Appraising her appearance in the mirror, she tried to remain calm when it came to Jess.

He's just a friend.

A really hot friend with a great backside.

She wouldn't mind putting her hands on that big chest of his either.

Or peeling his shirt off his chiseled body.

Get hold of yourself, Avery. You're doing research, not fulfilling fantasies.

She was eager to arrive at his place at the hour mark, but she forced herself to be ten minutes late. When he opened his door for her, he smiled down into her eyes. Her heart gave a happy skip, and she knew it was well worth the wait.

* * * * *

Christ, she was more stunning than he remembered, and Jess couldn't stop staring at her mouth. Her full lips looked as if she'd just eaten a pint of berries, and more than anything he wanted to swipe his tongue across them and taste her.

Instead of acting this out, he led her into his condo. The worst of the mess was hidden away—dirty clothes in the washer and his sheets changed. At least there weren't dirty dishes, and the floors were relatively clean. All it took to spruce up the place was plumping a couple of pillows on the gray sofa.

He stopped in the living room, and she looked around herself. "Nice place. Also, that's the longest sofa I've ever seen."

"I'm tall and like to stretch out."

"It's got four cushions instead of three. Did you have to special order that?"

He chuckled. "You'd be surprised what's out there if you're looking for it."

He found her smiling up at him. But closer study of her features revealed a hesitation in her eyes.

"Let me show you around, and we'll grab some drinks before digging in." He rubbed a hand over the back of his neck. "I admit I have no experience with ancestry research."

"If you have a few leads, we should be able to find a jumping off point."

He nodded. "C'mon." Having Avery in his house was making him feel edgy. His body was screaming for him to touch her, that there was an interesting, athletic and thoughtful woman within reach and his bed wasn't far off.

Lately, he'd taken any beautiful woman to bed. But with Avery, it wasn't only about wanting to abuse those lips of hers long into the night or plow between her strong thighs.

Christ, he wanted to stare into her eyes while he did it.

The notion didn't just scare him—he felt like a deer caught in the headlights. Each time he'd felt that strong pull to get closer to a woman, he crashed and burned.

She stepped up to the wall of big windows overlooking a personal terrace. From there, it led down several flights of steps to reach the community pool.

"This is a nice condo. The grounds are kept up beautifully, and I love the pool." Avery's comment roused him from his thoughts.

Jess watched her. She was still, not fidgety. At ease here with him. But he hadn't mistaken that concerned look in her eyes when he'd opened the door to greet her. Something was eating at her.

Same as him. They were one hell of a pair, weren't they?

He stepped up closer, gazing at her instead of the view of other condos with terraces overlooking the pool. "I like your hair today," he blurted.

She turned her head slowly, a light coming into her eyes. "Thanks. I just let it out of the ponytail. I probably wear one too much. I'm going to be one of those women with a receding hairline from having my hair pulled back. At work, I keep it tucked into a bun so nobody can make a grab for it."

As she spoke, she'd pivoted toward him. And Jess was damn good at reading body language. Very good.

She had a come-hither look to her, and he had to clench his fists at his sides to keep from grabbing her up and slamming his mouth over those sultry lips of hers... delving his tongue into her mouth and taking what he wanted. Giving her what she asked for with one simple look.

She dropped her gaze and then returned it to the view. "I bet you don't get out there to swim much."

"You're right. I work a lot, and I'm away from home."

She glanced back at him. "I saw that computer setup in your living room as we walked through."

What she referred to was the equipment he used to listen in to the phone calls between Moreno and his friends the system used to hack everything that was deemed un-hackable.

He gave an awkward chuckle and moved to the fridge rather than answer her. Pulling open the door, he looked inside. "I've got beer and sweet tea."

"A pale ale?"

"From a local craft brewery." He held up a bottle, and Avery's eyes lit.

"Oh, Reggie and I stop there sometimes."

Damn. Reggie wasn't the name of a beloved pet.

She came forward, and he handed a bottle to her. She expertly cracked it open and brought it to her lips as he did the same.

Shit—he had to know. "Reggie?"

She smiled. "My partner." Suddenly, her smile fell away and a crinkle cemented itself to her brow. "I saw him before coming over here. He said some things…"

God, Jess hated seeing her all twisted up this way. He fought to remain in place and not draw her into his arms, push her head down on his chest and assure her that he'd handle everything that came her way.

There it was—he was a protector by nature and most women didn't want anything to do with that.

Especially not a strong woman like Avery.

She glanced up at him, and whatever expression he had on his face gave her pause. "Reggie's married. Actually, he invited me over for burgers this weekend to visit with his wife."

"Ah."

Avery went on, "That isn't all he said, though. He told me more about the man I shot. His girlfriend…"

Seconds ticked by. Jess swallowed hard and stepped in. "Was pregnant."

She nodded.

"I heard." He reached out, his hand angling toward her cheek to cup her face, to feel if her skin was as soft as it looked. But he touched her arm instead. "You know you did the right thing, Avery. He made a move that was easy to mistake as a threat. You don't need to be ashamed for shooting that asshole—any one of us Rang—" He broke off. "Any law enforcement officer would have seen him reaching for his waist and taken the shot."

She set aside her beer and folded her arms over her chest. Looking up at him like his momma or one of his sisters-in-law would when he'd gone overboard and they wanted answers.

He looked back.

She arched her brow.

He gave a short laugh. "Shit. You caught that, huh."

She nodded.

"Grab your beer and come to my seven-foot-long couch so we can talk."

He just had to hold himself back from doing all the dirty things playing out in his fantasies since she'd walked through his front door.

Chapter Five

As Avery settled in one corner of the sofa with her beer in hand, her nerves hit. Sitting so close to Jess... God, was she sweating?

Being up close and personal with the bulge of his muscles and how his jeans strained across his thighs, something she didn't see when they were seated across from each other in a coffeeshop, she was definitely sweating.

He cast her a long look, as if sizing her up, assessing whether she could handle what he was about to tell her.

At this point, she wouldn't be surprised to hear he worked for the CIA. The man seemed to have information that the ordinary citizen wouldn't.

He pushed out a sigh.

She waited.

"Even though I told you, you would have probably guessed that my job deals with the law. But I'm not a city cop, a trooper or even a Texas Ranger — not anymore."

"You were, though," she said, sipping the beer that had a bright, crisp flavor.

He nodded. "Not that long ago either. A bunch of us Rangers were pulled from all over the state and given orders to raid this compound. Some radicals trying to kick up a fuss, a call to arms for the country and all that. In the end, we pulled together and took them down, and that got us recognized."

She nodded for him to continue.

"I work for a division of Homeland Security."

Her eyes widened with surprise. She hadn't expected that.

He gave a nod at her reaction. "Special forces units spattered throughout the country, and we make up the Southern Division."

"So you're the big guns, and it seems like I carry one of those cap guns that shoots a flag that says *bang*."

He shook his head. "Absolutely not. None of us are bigger or smaller. We're all in the same game, working for the same things. I just happen to handle…" He waved at his computer system. "…some darker shit," he finished.

She processed this for a moment, and he finished his beer. She watched his throat work with each swallow, and each swallow made her hotter for him.

"And your daughter? Where does she fit into all this? Did your wife disapprove of your choices?"

"Girlfriend at the time. And no, she approved. I was a state trooper, and she was young enough that she liked the spotlight that threw on her. She could tell her friends and family that she was dating a trooper, and it made her feel important. Things weren't that serious between us, but then she got pregnant and I offered to marry her. After that, I saw how she really felt about me, and that was she felt nothing at all. She refused my proposal and said she'd raise the child alone. I agreed..." He trailed off and pinched the bridge of his nose between thumb and forefinger.

Avery couldn't watch the struggle passing over Jess's rugged features and not make a move to comfort him. She scooted across the cushions toward him.

He dropped his hand. "I shouldn't have agreed to let her raise the baby on her own. I was stupid. Still am to have let it continue. But I backed off, agreed to stay on the fringes of Madison's life, because I didn't want to be that guy who pops in and out of her world when I wasn't working, which was too often to be consistent enough for a child. Anyway, none of it is a reason or even a good excuse. I was a shit, and I'm damn lucky Madison even approached me in that coffeeshop."

Avery rested a hand over his. When he turned his palm up and meshed their fingers, warmth seeped into her and a flutter started in her belly. "We're all human," she said. "And we can't always see the big picture at the time. But you're right that this is an opportunity to bridge the gap between you and Madison."

He nodded. "That's maybe more than I can hope for. But I'm going to do a damn good job on this project for her."

"And I'll help, if you'd like."

His stare intensified, and his throat worked once more. Then he moved close enough for her to touch. Or to slide into his lap.

Straddle him, grab him by the hair and kiss him.

She didn't move a muscle, even to breathe.

Slowly, he unlaced their fingers and lifted his hand to cup her face.

Oh God, she'd been wanting that touch so much, and she'd been thrashing herself for it for days.

His gaze burned into hers. "Know what I want?"

She couldn't breathe for the pounding of her heart. Shaking her head wasn't even a possibility, because she was frozen in place by that dark stare on Jess's face.

"This." He moved in.

His lips crashed over hers.

* * * * *

Fucking hell, she tasted like beer and woman and all the good things in the world. As Jess tangled his fingers into her hair and angled her head to give him deeper access, she moaned out, and he issued a growl in reply.

He swiped his tongue over hers, slow flicks that grew in strength. Each pass shooting his desire higher. His dick hardened, aching behind his fly. And if he didn't pull it out and shoot one off soon, his balls would explode.

"Jess..."

"Avery. Christ." He yanked her across his lap. She felt solid and warm, her hip and one buttock settled against his groin. He resisted the urge to grind his cock into her.

When she lifted a hand to his jaw and scuffed the pad of her thumb back and forth over the stubble growing there, the kiss took on a whole new dimension.

It went from bold, raw desire to heart-stopping tenderness.

He nibbled at her lower lip, sucked the soft flesh into his mouth. She moaned and flashed him a look that drew him to a complete halt.

Dammit. He couldn't go on and not risk his feelings. The game was fucking dangerous, there was so much at stake.

"Avery..."

She moved in his lap, throwing a leg over him and straddling him.

Fuck, her breasts were smashed against his chest, just begging for his hands.

A growl slipped from his throat.

He slid his fingers up her torso, giving her opportunity to pull away, but she arched into his touch. Fucking hell, he wasn't going to lose a woman he wanted to stay in his life just because he couldn't control his libido. Sex was a sure-fire way to end things forever.

But damn if he could control himself.

He *had to* control himself.

With a low groan, he grabbed her waist and pulled her up and off him. As soon as her backside hit the couch, he shot to his feet and took a step back. Then another. No distance was enough between them, and dammit, now he had to deal with the hurt look on her beautiful face.

"Hell, Avery, I'm sorry."

Her head was bowed, her chest heaving.

"I don't want to damage this friendship between us. I care about you too much."

She didn't respond.

Fuck, he was a cad. How selfish of him to kiss her and then leave her sitting there, nipples bunched, lips swollen... probably fucking wet for him. Obviously wanting.

"Say something."

She looked up at the grit in his voice. "You've got... a lot going on. So do I. It's best not to complicate things."

Hell, one look into her eyes and he wanted to scoop her up and carry her to bed. His muscles locked, threatening to make a move to do just that.

She ran her fingers through her thick brown hair. The sun streaming through the windows caught on the honey highlights.

"I'd still like to help you with the project. If you want…"

This was what friends did, right? Helped each other. There was no groping and stripping away clothes or moaning all night.

Friends had coffee and helped each other with kids' projects.

He pushed out a breath. "I'd like that. Very much."

I'd like to bury myself in you more.

She nodded. "Do you mind pointing me to your bathroom? I'd just like to…"

Finger yourself to ease the fire I just sparked inside you?

The thought of this beautiful woman sliding her fingers into her wet pussy while he was just a few walls away had his cock ramming itself against his fly.

"That way. Second door." He waved a hand. As soon as she walked out of the room, he dropped his face into his hand and rubbed at his eyes. But it didn't erase the image of her swaying hips from his mind.

* * * * *

Avery took one look into the mirror and flinched. Her hair was mussed, her lips swollen and a flush covering her throat.

Way to throw yourself at him.

He started it, she reminded herself.

But she hadn't wanted it to end. She'd thrown herself at him, ready to feel those rough hands all over her bare skin. Then he'd had to tear free of her.

"Ugh."

She could make excuses and leave. But that would threaten one of her only friends at this time in her life, and she felt Jess was too important for that.

She gave herself a little shake and washed her hands. After drying them, she smoothed some wild strands of hair and tried to make her heart slow in hopes of losing the redness in her cheeks.

After a minute or two, she felt more composed, ready to take on this project in the name of friendship.

When she walked into the living room, Jess looked up from his seat on the couch. He got to his feet and ran his fingers through his hair. The action was pure primal male, and it had her hot and panting for him in a blink.

Tearing her gaze from the bulging veins snaking down his forearm, she gave her best version of a serene smile. *No, nothing happened at all between us. No, I didn't want your fingers buried in my pussy and your tongue on my clit.*

91

Whatever this sharp attraction was, it had to be placed on the backburner. He'd friend-zoned her. And that was fine.

Wasn't it?

She told her body to shut up already and deal with it. Later, in bed, she may allow herself to remember the feel of Jess's hands on her so she could get herself off... but only once. Okay, maybe twice.

To her relief, he smiled back. And let the breath she'd been holding trickle from between her lips.

They stared at each other.

Damn that electric shock she felt each time his green and gold eyes landed on her.

"Uhh... do you have an ancestry site you prefer to start with?" she asked to break the tension mounting between them again.

When his gaze moved over her face, she sucked in sharply at the... The only way to describe his expression was animalistic. And hungry.

Her body responded, nipples peaking again and her body swaying, threatening to take a step toward him.

He gave a rough shake of his head that didn't match her question about his preference of ancestry sites. "I don't really have a clue. I've been so busy I haven't given it a lot of thought. What are my options?"

She gestured toward the computer system. "Why don't we start with a search? Or is this thing too high-tech for a simple search? I'm afraid it will tap into the Pentagon."

With a chuckle, he dragged up a second chair to the desk. Within minutes, they were combing through information. He typed a name, and it took Avery a second to look away from his hands and at the screen.

"That's my dad." When he turned his head to look at her, her stomach leaped.

"I see."

"I didn't grow up with him in my life. He took off before I have any memories of him. I'm a little nervous about what I might find on him, to be honest."

"Would you like me to do the reading on him?"

He shook his head. "I'm not that much of a wimp that I'd run from him. I mean… I storm bunkers and take down radical fundamentalists with thoughts to start their own militia. I can look into my own father, right?"

A smile spread over her face. "You really are the real deal, aren't you?"

He grunted. "I guess. All right, let's see what we find." He opened a search window, and an article popped up. As he skimmed it, she watched his face for a hint of a reaction. His face was a mask, and she wasn't able to tell if he'd discovered the right man or hit a dead end.

As time passed, she gave him some hints on keywords to search, and pretty soon they'd found Jess's paternal grandparents too.

He gaped at the screen. "Wow."

She inched to the edge of her seat. Excitement threaded through her. "I've never done this before. It's kind of fun. I might go home and look up my own history."

To her surprise, Jess pushed away from the desk. "Let's go grab a bite to eat and come back for more later. If you're up for it, that is."

Was this guy serious? He had to know how much she liked him. Even after he'd pushed her away, she was still here.

But only as a friend, and that was the way it should be. It was all so complicated for her right now, anyway.

She stood. "Thai food?"

He shot her a crooked grin. "I'm up for it. Let's go."

As she reached the front door, she felt a fleeting brush of fingertips over her spine as he guided her out of the condo. She felt the tingle of his touch all the way to the restaurant.

Over two Thai beers, light and cool, and plates of curry, spicy and filling, they chatted over everyday topics and steered clear of work. Avery was good with that, especially since she'd dwelled enough on her situation for one day. She'd been so stressed out that the few times she caught herself having a good time, she had to stop and think.

She could keep on feeling the nonstop guilt or allow her mind and spirit a reprieve. So she just sat back and listened to Jess talk about his mom and brothers growing up, letting her mind relax. Soon enough she'd be mulling over her situation again, right?

After they returned to Jess's place, they researched long into the night. She hardly remembered moving to the couch and didn't realize she'd dozed off until she woke. Startled, disoriented. A blue glow came from across the room, and the clock on her phone said it was past three in the morning. Jess still sat at the computer, eyes fixed on the screen.

She sat up. His devotion was… touching. For his sake and Madison's too, she hoped the project was a success. He hadn't told Avery so, but she knew he had his hopes riding on this bringing his daughter back into his life.

Moving slowly across the living room, she reached out a hand and rested it on his shoulder.

He looked away from the screen and gave her a small smile. "Guess it's late."

"I'm sorry I fell asleep. I thought I'd just sit down a moment, but the couch was comfy."

He pivoted his chair to face her. That brought his head to her waist level and when he gazed up into her eyes, she took a step closer to stand between his knees.

Silence ticked by the seconds. Then he bowed his head. Of their own will, her hands came around his nape, and she gathered him to her so he rested his head just beneath her breasts.

"God, Avery. I don't deserve the way you look at me," he grated out, muffled against her shirt.

The heat in his voice made her shudder, and he wrapped his arms around her middle and held her. When he looked up into her eyes, it was all over for her. A quiet rasp left her lips, and he shot to his feet, yanking her in and crushing his mouth over hers in the same movement.

The heady taste of man and desire flooded her brain, and she wiggled closer. The hardness of his body and the way he smelled drove her wild. Her panties grew damp as he pulled her roughly against him and drove his tongue into her mouth.

She scrabbled for a grip on his shoulders, and he lifted her as if she weighed no more than a piece of paper. He turned for his bedroom, and she didn't stop him no matter how much her brain was telling her she'd probably regret it. Each pace he took sent new shivers through her body. Her pussy clenched with anticipation.

As he strode to his bed, she broke the kiss long enough to look into his eyes. "Don't start something you can't finish," she whispered.

A noise in his chest made her nipples bunch with hunger. "I can fucking finish."

She locked her thighs around his hips, and he took a step to the bed. When he laid her down, covering her with his chiseled body, she let out a moan. Angling his head, he kissed her like he meant to set her on fire. Her body was already bursting into flames, but she wanted the inferno. She yanked him closer.

Kissing him, tugging at his clothes as he ripped her top off and cupped her breasts. The burning need inside her was stealing all her thoughts. She couldn't slow down. She had to feel him inside her.

She pushed on his chest, and he rolled into the covers, staring up at her with dark desire written on his rugged features. Straddling him, she put her hands on his bare, muscled chest, learning each inch of the hard work he'd put in right down over his six-pack abs.

He reached around her and with a flick of his fingers, unhooked her bra. It fell into his hands, and he tossed it away before clamping his fingers around her needy nipples.

Electricity shot through her, and she tossed her head back on a cry.

"Christ, you're beautiful. Tell me I'm not fucking this up."

"Only way you can fuck this up is if you don't make me come."

A grin stole over his face. "Don't you worry, baby."

He threw her down on the bed again and centered himself between her legs. Denim against denim wasn't enough for her, and she went for his waistband as he lowered his mouth to her throat, spattering kisses along her collarbones and then the tops of her breasts. When he took her nipple into his mouth, sweet torture claimed her senses.

*****

The ripe cherry of Avery's nipple on his tongue drove Jess closer and closer to the brink of insanity. There was no going back now—she'd made sure of that when she'd told him he'd fuck it up if he didn't make her come.

Challenge accepted.

He pulled on her sweet, succulent nipple with his lips and tongue. Then moved to the other. Back to the first one.

She guided him, her throaty moans driving him forward. He was battling not to focus on her hands at his fly. A single wrong brush of her fingers and he'd lose the game.

When she slid the zipper down and dipped her fingers into the elastic of his underwear, he caught her wrist in a hard grip.

She sucked in a gasp, eyes flaring with excitement.

"You like that? You like it rougher?" He saw something break in her eyes and her pupils dilated.

He closed his fingers around her wrist and jerked her hand up over her head, pinning it to the bed. Her breasts jiggled with the action that was just how he played in bed, but so many woman got turned on by it. He should know better than to use it on this woman.

Except it was *him*, the real him. And he was through pretending he didn't want her the way he damn well pleased and to hell with the consequences.

With one hand still locking hers to the bed, he leaned onto his knees to pinch her nipple.

She writhed under him, silent for now. But he could see she wanted to cry out in pleasure.

"Tell me what you like, baby. Do you like this?"

"I need..."

"Need it gentler?" His breath caught and held as he waited for her answer.

Her eyes drilled into his. "I need more."

"Jesus."

He tweaked her nipple until it stood out in a sharp peak, rosy red from the blood flow he'd brought to it. Then he strummed his fingers across her chest to the other nipple. When he was done with it, she had her head thrown back and her lips parted in a silent O.

He released her hand and gripped her waist as he lowered his lips to her smooth belly. He didn't exactly kiss a path down to her jeans—he placed nipping bites over her skin. Shit, he might be too rough, too anxious to be inside her to go easy.

"Jessss. I need you to touch me."

He jerked his head up, away from her stomach. Pink marks rose in the wake of his harsh kisses, along with red tracks from his beard stubble.

She made a noise of wanting, and he couldn't stop himself from tearing open her jeans and delving his hand into her panties.

Her. Very. Wet. Panties.

"Fuck," he bit off.

She pushed at her jeans, trying to get them down her hips so he could touch her.

He had to touch her.

When he yanked them off her, her panties came too, leaving her bared to him. The perfume of her musky desire shredded the last of his control.

He dropped his mouth to her pussy and drew on her clit. She came off the bed, hips rocking in the air as he found her hardened pearl and sucked.

She issued a rough moan that had his cock even harder. Maybe the hardest it had been... yeah, ever.

Stealing a look at her face, he watched ecstasy play over her features. The moment he saw her stomach dip and her mouth open wide, he almost came himself.

With a gentled stroke of his tongue over her clit, he toyed with her, bringing her down from the height he'd built her up to.

She shook in his grasp. As she was just learning this new side of his lovemaking, the soft kisses and swirls of his tongue dancing over her clit, he inched his fingers over her soaking seam.

Without warning, he drove his fingers inside. Hard. Deep.

And with a mission to make her scream.

* * * * *

Avery wasn't going to make it through the night if he kept making her heart palpitate this way. She'd die right here in Jess's arms on his bed, and damn if she cared.

She threw her legs wider apart to give him total access. Each thrust he made into her pussy with his thick fingers sent her up the bed a bit more. Each time he withdrew his fingers, her pussy clenched to keep them inside her.

He released a wild groan, and she grabbed at his hair. When she sank her fingers into the short, thick mass and tugged, he shot her a grin.

He doesn't mind rough play either.

The realization sent her into a new fit of fever. She pierced him in her gaze.

"Fuck me. Now."

"Yes, ma'am." His Texas drawl was all honey and promise, a complete juxtaposition to his jerky movements as he climbed off the bed and dropped his jeans and underwear.

She held her breath.

His cock bobbed on his washboard abs, purple with need and slightly arcing. She pushed up to lean on her elbows, eyeing Jess as she cupped his heavy balls in one hand.

He growled.

She ran her thumb over the base of his cock. "Get a condom."

If he minded her order, he didn't let on. He reached into his bedside drawer. In his hurry to get one out, the box flew out of his hand. Condoms scattered on the floor.

"We'll use 'em all up later," he said with a crooked grin that had her senses going haywire and her heart fluttering too.

When he reached for her again, she was shocked that he flipped her onto all fours with her ass up to receive him.

Leaning over her, he whispered in her ear, "Hold still while I enter you, baby. I don't want to come yet."

She trembled at his dark command and closed her eyes, waiting for him to move.

He glided his cock in hard and fast, hitting all the right spots along the way. She twisted the sheets underneath her and cried out. He rocked into her fast and then slow. Her mind barely caught up to the pleasure before he was pulling out of her body again and flipping her over.

When he cupped her ass and lifted her up to meet his thrust, she made the mistake of looking into his eyes… right as he slid home. Damn, her heart really was going to give out.

He slowed his pace and fucked her with a torture that had her pussy clamping down with a force that threatened a wicked finish.

Jess's gaze burned down into hers, and she lost herself on a wave.

"I'm coming," she cried out.

He claimed her lips, cutting off all sound as bliss sent her tumbling.

* * * * *

Every hard clench of her pussy around Jess's length, he ground deeper and clenched his jaw harder. Her body was so soft, so damn sweet, her curves filling his hands perfectly.

And hell if he was remotely finished with her.

Capturing her gaze, he churned his hips. Her cry cut off, and he caught her hands in one of his own and pinned her to the bed again. "Put your thighs around me."

She did.

"Fuck, the angle's goddamn heaven."

Her inner walls enveloped his cock, pulling at him until he felt a wildness come over him.

Slamming his mouth over hers, he delivered bruising kisses, which she returned stroke for stroke as he churned his hips. He bent his head and bit down on her nipple.

It was all she needed to throw her overboard into a third orgasm.

He followed with a roar, mind humming, body pulsing, cock shooting ropes of cum. Mind-numbing moments followed. Avery curled beneath him, holding him to her just as she had in the living room, the moment so tender it had wrenched his fucking heart.

He hadn't stopped himself from falling for those women before who weren't half as good as Avery.

Dammit, he couldn't stop it this time either.

It would end bad.

Her fingers threaded into the hair on the back of his head, and she latched him to her as they rode out the final aftershocks of their shared orgasm.

With his breaths rasping against her neck, he was aware he must be crushing her. *Just one more minute. One more minute to feel you all soft and warm under me before you leave my bed and never return.*

"Jess." Her murmur made him raise his head.

Her gaze burned into his, yanking on his fucking heart a second time. Shit. How many times had he thought himself in love before? This was the same—only lust. A mistaken belief Avery felt as deep in the moment as he did.

He was wrong, he knew it.

"Jess," she whispered again.

He found his voice. "Yeah, baby?"

To his shock, she cupped one breast and brought her hard gumdrop nipple to his lips. "I'm not convinced we did that right. Can we try again?"

Holy fuck. This was gonna hurt like a son of a bitch when she left him.

He took her nipple in his teeth.

Chapter Six

"Jess, a word." Sully's tone didn't give away what the conversation he wanted to have would be about, but Jess already knew—Moreno.

He stashed his boots into the bottom of his locker and closed the door.

Sully led the way into the conference room. Jess looked around. "What the hell happened in here?"

"New paint job," Sully said.

"And a table too. What happened to the old one?"

"Guess last time Colonel Downs was here, he thought the thing was a piece of shit and requisitioned us a new one."

Jess blew out a breath. "Does this mean OFFSUS is keepin' us around?"

Since the inception of the Ranger Ops team, it had been unclear whether or not a second special ops team in the South was actually necessary. Their jobs were always up in the air, but that didn't mean they cared any less. But job security sure would feel nice, and fixing up the headquarters might be a step toward that.

Sully sank heavily to one of the new chairs large enough to accommodate men as big as they were. "Not sure, but I'll take it. The table doesn't even creak anymore when you rest your elbows on it. Look." He demonstrated, and Jess chuckled, though he wasn't feeling amused at what was about to come.

What he suspected Sully would tell him was that they had what they needed to take out Moreno. For months, Homeland Security had been holding back that green flag, waiting to see what Moreno could give them.

The man had had more chances than a sinner at Heaven's gates to make things right and deliver intel to the right people and finally do some damn good in the world. Instead, he chose the wrong path every time.

"Look at this." He handed Jess a file.

Jess flipped it open and stared at the typed report. His head shot up. "Two hundred people. You're sure?"

"That's what they're saying. The intel provided by Moreno helped kill two hundred innocent victims in a town square who were there to see a visiting Catholic Cardinal."

"Shit." Jess sat back and rubbed his hand over his face. He was still exhausted after the night with Avery in his bed. Confused too, but he was putting that off for thinking about another time. Right now, he had Moreno on his mind.

"We stop this guy, we stop others. You know we've been waiting for something like this." Sully waited expectantly for Jess's reply.

He bobbed his head.

"It's just a matter of getting the intel from him first. Maybe we can stop further massacres like this."

Jess nodded again. "So a team on the ground. We go in and take him prisoner, pump him for information and then kill him."

"I think that's the plan. Though Homeland is considering waiting till he gathers all his cohorts in one place and then perform an air strike."

Jess was shaking his head. "We can't do that. It's risky. There are children and other innocent people surrounding him at all times."

Sully grunted. "That's what I said to Downs when he put it on the table. What are the chances of getting Moreno to leave his home for such a meeting?"

"Not sure. It would probably take an undercover there to persuade. Or pay off one of his own followers to turn traitor and make it happen."

"Good call. Any ideas who that kingpin could be?"

They talked for another half hour or so, and then Sully got to his feet. Jess stood too, and they faced each other.

He met Sully's gaze. "You know how I feel about taking out Moreno, but I want you to know that my judgment will not be clouded by the fact he's got kids. If I believe his number's up, we'll move on it."

He clapped Jess on the shoulder. "I know where your heart lies, man, and that's with your country."

Jess held out a fist, and they bumped knuckles. "I'll be on duty tonight."

"Let me know if you need anything."

After his commander walked out of the room, Jess drifted to the wall of windows and stared through the chink between the blinds. His thoughts were running full speed, through the tunnels of his mind like subway trains, making stops on various events or discussions. When his thoughts touched on Avery, that train came to a sudden halt.

It was impossible not to critically examine what had taken place between them the night before. So many times he'd fucked up with a woman, and that was the last thing he wanted with this particular one.

How she responded to him… fucking hell.

But he wasn't so naïve as to believe because sparks flew between the sheets that she was the right woman for him.

It was everything that had come before all that.

How supportive she'd been when Madison had approached him in that coffeeshop, and all the hours she'd put into the ancestry research. Offering moments of comic relief from the hours of digging through online archives and skim-reading newspapers for the names of his relatives. And how she hadn't even judged him for walking out of Madison's life in the first place, even though he deserved it.

He needed more time with Avery, uninterrupted where he could slow things down and maybe, just maybe, not make the same mistakes as he had in the past.

Only now he might be called out for a strike against Moreno. He could be gone for weeks, and any progress he'd made with Avery would be lost. In his experience, women didn't like to be kept waiting and would only put up with so many excuses.

Even though Avery probably understood his role more than others, she still wouldn't like being neglected. She was sexy, tough and smart, all the things men like Jess wanted in a woman. She could get so many guys who didn't take off for Mexico for weeks on end and could shower her in affection.

For the first time, he was considering dumping a woman before she dumped him.

He pushed out a sigh.

As he turned from the window, his phone buzzed. Down the hall, he heard a groan from one of the other team members as he also received the call. Then Sully's voice—"Gear up, bros. We're out in ten."

* * * * *

"Avery, can I talk to you a minute after class?" her kickboxing instructor called from the front of the room.

She nodded and reached for her water bottle. Sweat tracked down her spine, and she reveled in the cool liquid slipping down her throat to replace what she'd just worked out.

This was her third class in two days. With the incident in the parking lot still under review and Jess gone too, the workouts kept her going. For now.

After everybody had cleared out of the room, she slung a towel around her neck and approached the instructor. He lowered his water bottle from his lips and grinned at her.

Big, built and sexy, the instructor was the reason so many women took the class. If Avery hadn't met another guy who pumped her up even more than this one, just with a single look, she might have drooled over him too.

"You really kicked some ass this week," he said.

"Thanks. I enjoy a challenge."

"That's what I wanted to talk to you about."

She arched a brow.

"I have a week away planned, my uncle's seventieth birthday in Omaha."

"Omaha? I could think of more exciting destinations," she teased.

He chuckled. "I know. But it's the location. So I've got my ticket paid for, but I have a problem you could help me solve."

"I'm listening."

"What would you say to taking over my classes for a week?"

She blinked at him.

He rushed on, "I know it's probably an odd request."

"It's true I've never heard that one before."

"You're the only person I know who can handle two classes a day and keep their stamina up to lead the classes. You'd be paid by the gym, and they'll offer you a free membership for a year."

"That's a great opportunity. Thank you for considering me."

He cocked his head. "Please tell me you'll do it."

"For your uncle in Omaha, yes. I'll do it."

He embraced her. Briefly, she hugged him in return and then pulled away. "I'm sorry I'm all sweaty."

"So am I," he said. "Doesn't bother me a bit. Thanks for agreeing to do this. I can stop worrying about it now."

"I'm glad to help. And that free membership doesn't sound so bad."

He laughed. "Maybe when I get back from the party, we could go for drinks after class."

She eyed him. This wasn't her first rodeo, and she'd been asked out enough times to know that expression in her instructor's eyes wasn't purely gratitude for taking over his classes. Two months ago, she might have been happy to see where a date with him would lead, but now not so much.

Still, it was just a drink, and she nodded in agreement. Maybe it was the fact she hadn't heard from Jess in seven days or just making new friends that made her agree to it.

"Great, I'll let you know the class schedule tomorrow," he said.

"Thanks." She threw him a wave and walked away, her mind already shifted from teaching a kickboxing class or drinks with a hot instructor to other issues.

Such as wanting to date a special operative who'd made it clear he didn't want more. She'd gone to bed with Jess despite knowing this, and still she didn't have regrets. Whenever she thought of that night, her skin still came alive with tingles where his hands had been… his lips had been.

His teeth had been.

He'd excited her beyond anything she'd known before, shot her into a new realm of sexual play that wouldn't be matched for a long time to come.

Jess hadn't only taken over her body—her emotions were involved.

She knew he was away with Ranger Ops, and that didn't bother her. She could deal with him coming and going without notice. The problem was her wanting to add feelings to the mix, letting him know she cared and prayed he came home safe.

Those weren't the feelings of a woman who only wanted one night of passion.

She quickly showered in the locker room and changed. When she walked out of the building, she bumped into the instructor again, and he offered to walk with her since he was headed that direction too.

Their talk was carefree with no pressures. She didn't dump all her problems in his lap the way she had with Jess. Was that a good thing or bad?

Only thing she knew was how hung-up she was on Jess, even in such a short time period. She should probably try to rein that in.

When she and the instructor said their goodbyes, she felt no pang of sadness for it to be ending so soon. She just didn't feel anything at all for the man.

She'd talked herself into not texting Jess after their interlude. But thinking on it now, maybe it was a mistake—it might have showed him that she didn't care. A warm word, letting him know someone cared about him and appreciated his service wouldn't be a bad thing, right?.

Once she reached her apartment, she dropped her gym bag to take care of later and pulled out her phone.

Ten options ran through her mind.

I like spending time with you.

No, that was corny. Might as well buy a greeting card.

I want you between my legs again.

Maybe that was slutty? Was there such a thing with a guy as hot as Jess Monet?

She settled for *thinking of you,* and after she sent the text wished she could pull it back out of cyberspace. Too late to dwell on it, she went about her business of cleaning up, paying some bills online and the weekly phone call to her parents.

Then she settled down with her computer tablet to read the daily news. A story on current world events popped up, and she sat straighter as she read.

Apparently, a threat had been neutralized just off the Gulf Coast, where a ship had been blown up and capsized. Ten crew members and passengers had been rescued, and then the government seized ten thousand pounds of cocaine headed for the US.

She set aside her tablet to process this. This was exactly something Jess would be involved in, wasn't it? Could he have been responsible for sinking that ship? Or for the rescues?

Picking up her tablet again, she spent some more time scrolling and found a grocery store ad for half-price pork ribs, which got her thinking about whipping up some barbecue and how much her fellow officers raved about it. Before she knew it, she

115

had an idea in her mind. Perhaps it would keep her from the dreaded boredom or maybe it would show Jess how much she appreciated him, even if it was only from a friend stance.

She was going to plan a barbecue for him and his team. And his daughter and her mom, if they agreed to come too.

* * * * *

Jess got behind the wheel of his Mustang and grabbed for his phone. Dawn was just breaking over the city, and he was fucking dead on his feet. But he didn't want to waste a single moment he could be talking to Avery.

Finally, he understood why the other guys on the team sometimes got quiet and retreated to their own thoughts. Hell, he'd thought about her nonstop, and all he wanted was a hot shower, a steak and Avery in his bed. Then a big order of Chinese while they worked on his daughter's project.

As soon as he switched on his phone and saw her short message, his heart gave a hard flex.

She was thinking of him. Or had been less than a day ago.

He considered texting back or calling. In the end, he brought the cell to his ear.

"Jess." Her tone sounded… happy. She was happy to hear from him.

Well, this was new for him.

116

He caught himself grinning. "Hi, Avery. I got your text."

"Oh. It was nothing."

Nothing? Or *nothing*?

He was overthinking. He had to make a move on her or let her go forever to join the dozen other women he'd once believed he felt something for.

"I'm in the city and I'd like to see you," he said.

"I'd like that too." A smile entered her voice. "In fact… I wondered if I threw a little party if you might want to bring your teammates."

Surprise hit him. "What kind of party?"

"I made a massive batch of barbecue. It's been outside on my balcony in the smoker all night long. The meat's falling off the bone."

He groaned, his stomach cramping with hunger at the thought of anything besides made to eat military rations. "Love to. And I'm speaking for them because believe me, they'll want a meal that sounds that good. How many can you fit in that apartment of yours? Never mind—make it my place. I'll come over and help you bring the barbecue here."

She laughed, and the sound swallowed Jess. For a dizzying minute, he could only think of her after he'd just given her an orgasm, when she was relaxed and glowing with pleasure and happiness. He wanted to see her like that every damn day.

Shit—too deep. Way too deep, buddy.

It was beyond the point of return.

"I'll get the meat and sauce all packaged up. I have some potatoes for a salad too. And cornbread."

He moaned again. "You're mighty tempting to a man who's just eaten dried chicken patties for three straight days. Let me go home and grab a shower and I'll come over."

Silence greeted him. Then, she said, "You know I've got a shower too, Jess."

Fuck. She wasn't messing around, and his cock was registering the fact by standing at attention with a boner of salute.

"I'll be right over then."

"Good."

He paused, wondering if he should warn her about his appearance. He and the rest of the team were always banged up and sporting injuries from their missions. In the end, he didn't tell her. He'd explain once she opened the door and saw him face-to-face.

In minutes, he arrived at her apartment. Looking up at the front of the building, he wondered what Avery had been doing while he was away. After touching US soil, he hadn't had a moment to check into her review. For all he knew, the badge was back on her uniform. He hoped to hell it was.

He sat there another minute, thoughts roaming over Avery. She wasn't playing hard to get or pushing him away—at least not yet. He couldn't figure her out, and that threw him the most.

In his career, he was both a lock, allowing no threats past him, and a lockpicker that figured out others. But he didn't know how to move forward with Avery. To break her open and show her how she could feel with him or to let her get close enough to break into him? Problem was, he was pretty sure he'd already let her do that.

In the end, he realized he was analyzing it overly much. That part of him that dug into intel and cracked codes, evaporated the smoke screens shielding people from the truth, was trying to use that in life. But life, thank God, was much simpler.

He walked up to her building, and she buzzed him in. As he navigated the stairs, it was impossible for him not to see places a person could ambush Avery and cause her harm.

He told himself she could take care of herself.

When he knocked on the door, she opened it immediately. Taking one look at his battered face and the line of stitches across his brow, she gave a small shake of her head. Stepping back, she allowed him inside and closed the door.

"You gonna lock that?" he asked, voice suddenly grittier than it had been.

"It locks automatically."

They stared at each other. Then she stepped forward at the same moment he opened his arms to her.

She went on tiptoe to press a gentle kiss to the only part of his face that didn't feel bruised—his lips.

When her sweet flavors enveloped his brain, he issued a growl of desire and yanked her flush against him. She gently spun her arms around his neck. "I don't want to hurt you."

"Worst is over. Just looks bad now." He searched her eyes. The lights playing in the depths was killing his desire to go slow.

She slid her hand over his shoulder and downward to entwine her fingers with his. She gave a small tug on his hand. "Let's hit the shower."

He'd never been in her apartment before, and he hardly cared about anything but looking at her. The way her ass looked when she leaned into the shower to switch on the water. How her hair started to curl on her shoulders from the steam.

Reaching for him, she moved to strip away his clothes. He stood completely still and let her peel off his civilian clothes. When she discovered his sidearm tucked against his spine, she didn't flinch and simply set it aside on the bathroom countertop.

"The perk of having a girlfriend who's a cop," he said before he considered what he was saying.

Her gaze flew to his, and her lips fell open. "Am I your girlfriend?"

"Fuck, Avery. I can't pretend with you." He cupped her face in his hands and angled closer so their lips were a breath apart. "I want you to be."

* * * * *

He was inside her before they even got into the shower. His thick cock stretching her walls as he tongue-fucked her mouth with deep, slow strokes.

He hitched her thigh higher on his hip, driving in and out in a rhythm that was set to undo her.

Shaking with desire, she rocked into him. His length speared her, and she let out a gasp. Need ratcheted higher. For a week, she'd been trying to find some inner peace, something to sweep her away, and this was it. No amount of kickboxing classes or jogs in the park were doing what she'd needed all along—Jess.

He lifted her, and she wrapped her arms around his neck. Their lips crashed together, and he remained joined with her as he stepped into the shower. The warm spray washed over them, darkening his hair. She lifted her fingers to the strands.

When he pressed her spine against the shower wall and tore from the kiss, she looked into his eyes. The same dark passion she felt was reflected in the depths of his gaze.

With a growl, he took her lower lip between his teeth and worried it back and forth gently as he churned his hips. His swollen head of his cock bumped the perfect spot, and she dug her fingers into his shoulders to lever herself into him.

"Fuck, you're so damn deep," she grated out.

121

"I amend my statement—I fucking love having a girlfriend who's a cop."

She threw her head back with both pleasure and amusement. "Why?"

"Because you're just as foul-mouthed as I am, and it's hot as hell in bed."

"We're in the shower."

He answered with a groan that raised the hairs along her arms. With one hand cupping her ass, he slipped the other between their bodies. As soon as the big pad of his thumb depressed her clit, shockwaves ran through her. Those vibrated her core, and she crushed her lips down over his as the first pulsation hit.

Jess claimed her mind and body with each thrust of his cock. Her muscles tensed and released around his shaft. The moment she felt him let go, she opened her eyes and stared into his.

He came on a loud roar. The throb of his cock triggered her pussy to contract harder around him. As passion captured her heart, she dropped her forehead against his. He thumbed her clit once more, and she shuddered. When he let her slip down his body, he held her up for a moment while she regained her senses.

"Jess..."

He tipped her chin up with his knuckles and searched her eyes. Without a word, he kissed her. The tender brushing of his mouth over hers set her heart aflutter.

He broke the kiss and enveloped her in his strong arms. They stood there holding each other while the water rained down on them.

Then she lifted her head from his chest and they shared a smile.

Chapter Seven

Jess's condo was packed inside and out. A keg was tapped and party cups passed around. And the scent of barbecue was heaven.

His stomach cramped at the scent, and he weaved his way through the group of friends to where Avery stood at the counter, pulling apart the ribs to make small portions. Her back was to him, her hair over one shoulder to expose her neck.

As he approached, Lennon caught his eye and grinned knowingly. Jess gave only a chin nod in return and settled his hands on Avery's hips. She glanced over her shoulder at him and smiled.

God, this felt good. Coming home after a long mission always did, but having somebody to come home *to* was even better. Add in the big gathering of friends, sharing food and good times, and he couldn't remember when he'd last been this happy.

"Is it ready now? I'm starved."

She nodded, and then sighed as he pressed a kiss to her neck.

"Hey, save it for later, man," Lennon called out.

Jess gave him the finger.

Avery turned in his arms and hugged him. Just as quickly, she stepped back. "What's the time?"

"Six-ish. Why?"

She grabbed his hand and towed him through the kitchen into the living room. There his buddies from the Ranger Ops and their wives or girlfriends took up the sofa. Drink cups littered the surface of his coffee table.

Avery threw them all a wave, and it warmed Jess to know she wasn't shy at all.

"Hey, your girl knows how to put on a party," Sully said from his comfortable position on the sofa with his arm slung along the back. Next to him, his wife was curled up close.

"Thanks," Avery sang out as she passed. "Food's on, so grab a plate."

"Damn, I've been smelling that barbecue for twenty minutes, and my stomach's been rumbling. I'm ready." Sully got up and pulled Neveah with him. "Hey, Jess, thanks for having us over, but we've gotta head out as soon as we eat. The babysitter has to leave early."

"No prob, man. Glad you could come." Though he'd just spent days with these people, he still felt the brotherhood burn strong. He and Sully clapped each other on the backs in a bro hug that had their woman giving them amused grins.

Behind him, Jess heard a faint knock at the door and turned. Avery quickly strode across the room to open it. What he saw had his knees feeling weak.

His daughter walked in, with her mother right behind.

The air sucked out of the room, and his mind blanked as he set eyes on Madison's precious face.

He lurched forward to greet her, heart pumping hard. "Hi, Madison."

"Hi." She looked nervous—just as nervous as he felt. Beside her, Jenna placed a hand on her shoulder to ease her into the space, which luckily emptied since everybody went to the kitchen for food.

"Thanks for inviting us," Jenna said.

"I'm glad you came," he said genuinely, not looking away from his daughter's face.

She gave him a small smile.

"I'm sorry I'm not finished with my end of the family tree project yet. I've been away and—"

"It's okay," she broke over him. "It isn't due till the end of the month."

"Okay, good. Do you want to get something to eat? We can go out back and sit and talk." He threw her mother a look to make sure that was okay. When she nodded, Madison did too.

"C'mon." Jess resisted the urge to put an arm around his child and lead her away and instead just waited for Madison to follow.

He tossed a look over his shoulder to see Avery and Jenna standing together, talking. Warmth and affection spread over him. Avery had set aside any awkwardness she may feel at inviting his ex, in order to get Madison here.

The woman was fucking amazing.

As he and Madison got into line to fill their plates, he caught his friends shooting them questioning looks. He'd be doing a lot of explaining later, but right now, he just wanted to spend some time alone with his kid.

It was funny watching the choices Madison made—ribs were a yes on her plate, but she skipped the baked beans, which weren't his favorite either. Though he did take a small scoop to make Avery happy. Then he held the back door open for her to go out onto the terrace.

They were alone, and it was quiet out here. Suddenly, he felt all jammed up. How did a father even speak to a daughter he didn't know and never saw?

To his surprise, the conversations he'd overheard between Moreno and his children sprang to mind. He asked them about their day, their chores, their schoolwork. He sank to a chair next to Madison, and it stunned him how easy it was to strike on a topic that interested her.

He listened to her tell him about soccer and her friends. How she was considering not playing next year, because she was interested in volleyball. He encouraged her by asking more questions.

Pretty soon, they were laughing and joking around. If he thought on it hard, he'd feel tears burn at the backs of his eyes—he'd wanted this for so fucking long and always felt it was out of reach.

But it had taken one step from Madison and then an overture from Avery and everything was looking toward a future for him and his daughter.

"Can I get you another drink?" he asked.

"No thanks. I should probably see what Mom's up to. We can't stay all that long—my friend's having a birthday party today too."

"Oh. Well, do you need a little cash to buy her a gift? I could—" He reached for his wallet.

Before he pulled it out, she stopped him with a smile. "Thanks, but I already got her something with my allowance money."

"Ah. All right."

They stared at each other. A lump leaped into his throat.

"You know, Madison, I've really enjoyed this. And I'm sorry I waited so long to make it happen."

She studied him in silence.

"I hope we can do it more often. Maybe you can take my phone number too. That way you can get in touch with me whenever you want. Just know that sometimes I'm not always around to answer."

She nodded. "My mom told me. But yeah, that'd be cool."

His chest loosened a bit as they exchanged numbers. Finally, he followed her back to the front door and her mother stood as they entered the living room. Avery shot Jess a look, and he gave her a nod. *Everything's good. Thank you for this.*

She returned his look with a gentle smile, her heart in her eyes.

Jess turned to Madison's mom. "Thank you for coming. For letting her come here."

"It was time. Wasn't it, sweetie?" She slipped an arm around Madison, and Jess felt himself burning to do the same.

"After I finish my research on my side of the family, maybe I could see you again? To exchange the information?" He cocked a brow at Madison.

She smiled, all sweet and gawky teen rolled into one. And he couldn't be prouder or think her more perfect. "I'd like that."

"All right then. Good. I'll be in touch." He squeezed her shoulder. Then said to hell with it and pulled her into his arms. She felt fragile and solid at the same time, and the lump was lodged in his throat again.

Madison brought her arm around him. Over her head, he saw Avery twist away and wipe her eyes. He gave his daughter one last squeeze and then released her.

"Bye," she said to him, and then she and her mother left.

He and Avery stared at each other.

"I hope that was okay," she said. "I should have asked you first, but it was a snap decision and I just thought—"

He caught her in his arms, silencing her with a kiss. She melted into him. After a long moment, he pulled back and gazed into her eyes. "Thank you for that, baby. It was…" Words evaded him, and he gave up trying to find some.

Avery smiled. "I'm glad you enjoyed each other."

"It's long overdue," he said. "But I won't let that happen again."

She rested her head on his chest. "I'm happy for you."

"And another thing."

She straightened to look at him.

"If you ever decide to leave the police force, you've got a hell of a career as a barbecue pit master."

She tossed her head back and chuckled. Jess kissed her open mouth.

* * * * *

Avery leaned on one elbow, her head cradled on her palm as she used the other to stroke Jess's bare chest. Maybe it was a bit of an infatuation she was

130

experiencing, but she felt as if she couldn't quit touching him.

And there was so much of him to explore. He was tall and broad, muscled in places she'd never seen men muscled in. When she traced down his abs and around to his hip, she let her fingers flutter on a band of muscle in the crease where his abs and thigh met.

He cracked an eye and peered at her. "Like what you see?"

"There's a lot to admire."

"On you too." He rolled onto his side and faced her. As she gripped his hip around to his carved ass, he grabbed hers too, tugging their naked bodies flush. She sucked in a breath at the heated touch of flesh on flesh.

"I can tell you work hard for this body." His low rumble pebbled her nipples, which of course, he noticed. He slipped a hand up to cup her breast, his thumb moving back and forth in a maddening fashion.

"All I've had so far in this review is a psych eval, so lately working out is all I've got. I've attended so many kickboxing classes that the instructor asked me to be his substitute the next few weeks while he's away."

A grin cut over Jess's face. "That's great. When do you start?"

"I haven't been given a start date yet." She lifted a shoulder and let it fall, but she might have moved her arm to give him better access to her breasts.

Which again, he noted, and pressed her gently onto her back to tease each. Every twist of his fingers had her pussy slicker with desire, and soon she was gasping and arching off the bed.

He watched her with a light in his eyes that she wasn't sure how to interpret. It seemed as though a switch had been flipped in him. In days, he'd gone from pushing her away, holding her at arms' length, to admitting he wanted her in his life.

When he lowered his mouth to one nipple, she came off the bed with a soft cry. With a hand on his nape, she guided him over her breasts and then applied pressure to direct him downward where she wanted him most.

He scraped his stubbled jaw over her lower belly to her mound. As he parted her thighs, he looked up at her. "Feel free to scream, baby."

"Don't worry. I won't hold back." She flashed a grin, which was quickly wiped away by a gasp as his wet tongue flattened over her clit.

Tingles spiraled out over her body, enveloped every inch. He sucked at her clit with strong pulls and just when she began to crest, he'd back off with nibbles and light flicks of his tongue.

She grabbed at his shoulders and did something she never thought she'd hear coming from her own mouth — begging.

"Jess… please. Oh God. Don't stop that. Ohhhh damn."

He vibrated a chuckle against her pussy, which only heightened her pleasure.

"You're going to… get the same teasing in re—turn!" Her words broke on a hiccup of satisfaction as he gave her what she wanted and sucked her clit between his lips.

Ecstasy stole all sense of thought. After only seconds, she was peaking, thrusting her hips upward and spilling her juices on every contraction he pulled from her.

At some point, he slowed his licks and she collapsed onto the bed. He held her with his arms wrapped around her hips and his jaw resting on her mound. Looking up at her, he smiled.

She moaned in bliss.

"Good?" he asked softly.

"You couldn't tell? By all means, try again." She nudged him toward her pussy.

He laughed. "I thought you were planning to return the teasing favor."

She'd barely recovered from that heart-stopping orgasm, but she wasn't going to back down from this challenge. Sitting up, she rolled atop him and kissed him long and deep. Her own flavors rode on her tongue, and she'd never felt so beautiful or sexy or desired than by this man at this minute.

She slipped down his body, kissing and leaving small bites across hard pecs, the ridges of his abs, down to those yummy hip muscles. As she dipped her head to take his cock into her mouth, he drew her hair over her shoulder.

"I wanna watch."

God, even his dark words thrilled her to the core. She pressed her thighs together and learned how he felt in her mouth.

Swirling her tongue over the mushroomed head, down the thickened shaft over veins and straining length to the base. From there, she mouthed down to his sac. He grunted out his pleasure, and she reveled in the sound. She moved back up, teasing over and over until he gripped her hair in his fist.

"Suck me."

The command pulled a mewl from her lips.

She looked into his eyes as she took him into the back of her throat. He rocked upward, sinking deeper, holding her by the hair, and damn, that shouldn't be sexy but it was the biggest turn on.

She moved restlessly against the bed, needing to feel him sinking deep into her and the light tug on the strands of her hair just before he claimed her lips.

Wanting to take him to the brink as he'd done her, she let his cock go with a soft *pop* of her lips. Then she curled her fingers around it, smoothing her thumb over the wetness pooling at the tip.

"Dammit, I was so close."

"I know," she said with a coy smile.

"That's it, woman." He reached down and yanked her up under the arms. Then with her straddling him, he grasped her hips and rubbed his cock over her soaked folds. "We'll see who can tease better."

Without thought, she bore down on him. His cock slipped inside her in one hard thrust.

She went still, shock flaring her eyes wide. "No condom."

"Fuck. I've never had a woman bare before." He squeezed his eyes shut on a moment of bliss, and then opened them. "Even with Madison, it was a broken condom. Shit. Let me get one."

He drew her up and off him. She rolled into the sheets and watched as he slammed a rubber over his impressive length with a swift jerk of his wrist. Biting her lips, she spread her thighs wide in invitation.

"Look at that wet pink pussy. I'm going to fuck it good."

She loved his dirty pillow talk as much as what he was about to do to her. Reaching for his shaft, she guided him between her legs. He claimed her with one thrust of his hips, and then they were moving fast and hard toward an end neither was willing to waste a second of.

Grabbing at his ass, she raked her blunt nails across his chiseled muscle. He sucked on her neck, leaving her writhing. The swell of pleasure was riding toward her, about to encapsulate her.

When he growled out his release, she tipped over the edge too. Tumbling through emotions and sensations until she realized she'd forgotten to breathe.

* * * * *

"Great class, Avery. Thanks."

She looked up at one of the women wiping perspiration off her neck in the front of the room and smiled. "You've really improved the past few days. Got the moves down."

"Yeah, it took me a bit, but I really enjoy working with you." She smiled and grabbed her weighted gloves to stuff into her bag. Then she threw Avery a wave and left the room.

She sighed. Doing a good job at the kickboxing class—and being told so—came with a feeling of depression as well. She wanted to be recognized as a good cop. Instead, she was being strung along and told the investigation was taking longer than usual because all the board members must be present, and they seemed to be gone more than not. Add in the review of her entire life, including every takedown and arrest she'd made, and she was stuck.

Stuck, stuck, stuck.

And she was pissed.

Her patience had been cuffed and stuffed, and now she wanted to break free of the shackles of this review. Today she was getting answers, even if she had to hunt down each and every board member in their homes. Hell, she didn't care if she interrupted dinners or backyard baseball games with their kids or even if they were in the bathtub—she was getting an answer. Today.

She ran home to shower and dress in something more fitting for paying a visit to the precinct. As soon as she walked through the doors, she was greeted by happy smiles and greetings of welcome.

Her heart warmed. This was her home—her job was her world. And it had been wrenched from her for an error any one of them would have made.

"I'd like to see Chief Gilbert," she said to the receptionist.

She nodded. "I'll tell him you're here, Avery."

"Thank you."

"When do you think you'll be back?" she asked Avery.

"That's what I'm here to find out."

"Is that Officer Aaron's voice I hear?"

She craned her neck to see the man attached to that voice—her partner Reggie.

He came out into the reception area, a grin on his face. Avery couldn't help but return it. It was so good to see him. The longing to return to the beat, to patrol the city was strong enough to choke her up.

Reggie saw it. After working closely together for two years now, he knew her moods like a brother.

"Oh, hey. You must really miss me. We never did have those burgers, did we? This weekend. The missus asked about you just yesterday."

"Yeah? At least I'm not forgotten."

"C'mon." He twitched his head toward one of the interrogation rooms.

She threw a look at the receptionist. "I'll be with Reg if the chief comes looking for me."

"Of course, Avery."

Reggie led the way into a small room containing a table and a few chairs. There was a place to shackle the prisoner to by the cuffs, and she avoided sitting there, moving around the table instead.

Chuckling, Reggie sat in the prisoner's spot. "I'm not afraid," he said in his deep bass.

She laughed. "I have no reason to be afraid either. So..." she placed her palms on the tabletop "...any news on the victim? The press isn't saying jack shit, and I'm not allowed any information, it seems. All my calls are going unanswered over here."

Reggie sat back in the chair to eye her. "You look different, Avery," he said, ignoring her questions.

She blinked. "Different how?"

"I don't know." He waved a hand at her appearance. "You look…" He swirled his hand in the air over his face. "You're glowing or something."

God. She was glowing? It had to be Jess's doing. After several orgasms the previous night, she had barely been able to pry herself down from the cloud she'd been on this morning.

"Is it a man?" Reggie leaned in, that gleam in his eyes.

There was no point in lying to her friend. Nodding, she said, "I'm seeing someone new."

"New? Hell, when was the last time you dated at all, Aarons? I'm proud of you for getting out there. You deserve a piece of that happiness, someone to come home to and wash away the day's hardships."

"Maybe." She chewed on her lip.

"Oh now, you know I'm right. You aren't a bad person, and you're far from a bad cop. You got yourself into the wrong place at the wrong time is all, and any of us would have shot that dude in self-defense."

Her chest felt as though something heavy sat atop it every time there was mention of what had happened at the grocery store that night. "I know. I stand behind my defense."

"Damn straight."

"And that's why I'm here — to ask Chief about my review. Do you know what's going on with it, Reg?"

He pushed out a rough sigh. "I don't. Wish I did, but they're keeping it locked up tighter than a nun's chastity belt."

A smile traced across her face at Reggie's colorful expression. "I miss the hell out of your sayings, Reg. You always make me laugh."

"Well, somebody's putting more than smiles on your face, that's clear. Who is he? That state trooper who always eyeballs you when he steps into the city limits?"

"No, not him. It's not anybody you know. His name's Jess."

"Well, Jess is a pretty lucky man. Tell him he'd better not hurt my partner or he'll be answering to me."

That roused a chuckle from her. "I don't think I'll tell him that, but I appreciate the brotherly love." She opened her mouth to say more, when the door opened, and they were interrupted by the chief himself.

He looked between her and Reggie. She shot to her feet. "Chief Gilbert."

He gave a nod. "Aarons, Maples."

Reggie stood and moved toward the door to go. Gilbert held up a hand. "You might as well stay, Reg. She'll tell you what I have to say anyway. Cuts out the middle man."

Reggie returned to his seat, and the chief sank to one as well. Her stomach blooming with butterflies, Avery sat down.

The chief met her stare. "You know there's not much I can tell you, Avery. I wish I could."

"Is my case even being reviewed? Or is it all on hold?"

"Some discussions have taken place. Your latest psych eval has been sent to us in a report."

Great—she couldn't wait to learn what they thought of her now. As if it wasn't bad enough believing fate had been gunning for her and she was destined to die at the hands of a criminal, those crimes would now be used against her. It was all up to the board, of course, but right now she wasn't feeling very optimistic.

Reggie tossed her a look. "Chief Gilbert, give it to us straight. I want to go back out on those streets with my partner at my side. When will Officer Aarons be reinstated?"

"Soon we'll have a decision, I'm sure. Within the month."

"The month?" she cried out before she could squelch her reaction to the news.

He nodded. "These things take time. You can use this time to get your head on straight. Take the counseling that's been offered. Maybe attend some anger management classes."

She shot to her feet so fast that her chair slid across the floor. Reggie let out a groan, knowing her anger was hitting full force and when that happened, there was as much chance of stopping it as a man stopping a tractor-trailer with his bare hands.

Her hands shook, and she clenched them into fists at her sides. "I do not have anger problems, Chief. I was faced with a choice back in that parking lot. I chose not to get shot. Even though it turned out the assailant didn't have a weapon, I defended myself, same as you would. Or Reggie. Or any damn cop in this precinct. I didn't have a wave of anger come over me and just felt like shooting a guy in the chest."

The chief didn't respond, only stood and moved to the door. "Even if that isn't the case, Aarons, take the course. It will look better on your record."

As soon as he walked out, closing the door behind him, Avery let out a low, "Fuuuuuck."

Reggie moved around the table to grip her shoulder. "Don't let it all get to you. It's protocol, and following it will only help your cause."

"Fine. Whatever. I'll do it. Right now, I've gotta run. I can't be late for kickboxing."

Reggie yanked her in for a hug, and she patted his back in return, fighting off a swell of true anger at the situation. No answers. Just more waiting. And her being blamed for something based on what had happened to her in the past.

* * * * *

Jess could decode the most sophisticated intelligence. He'd examined letters between Moreno and a group of extremists out of Mexico City. And he'd listened to so many phone calls that his mind was nothing but a roster of the names of people he didn't know personally and who wouldn't likely live to see the new year.

All of this was Jess's everyday life.

But damn if he could figure out what was eating at Avery.

He turned from the computer monitor and scrubbed at his grainy eyes. Six solid hours of staring at words and numbers, trying to draw lines between a recent bombing in Buenos Aires and the man he was after, and he could use a break.

He could use a little lovin' from his girlfriend, if he was honest. But Avery had been silent and sullen all night, giving him monosyllabic answers via text.

Picking up the phone, he hit a button to video chat her.

She picked up right away, and when he saw she was propped against pillows in bed, his gut clenched with desire. He should be there with her. Instead, he was a dog chasing its tail on this shit with Moreno.

"Jess, it's late. Are you still up working?" she asked.

"Just wrapping up for the night. But why are you up?"

"I was reading." She lifted a book in front of the screen so quickly he didn't get a good look at the title.

"What would you say about some company?" He held his breath after asking the question — he was still damn gun-shy about putting his feelings out there. But with Avery, it was getting easier.

She nodded. "Come on over."

He saw the pinch of worry between her brows and wondered if he'd been the one to put it there. Somehow he didn't think so — it was more likely the thing that had kept her quiet and withdrawn all evening and into the night.

"Be there in a while, baby."

He hadn't even made it to the car when his phone buzzed. The text from Downs made him groan. Locking himself inside his car, he stared through the dark windshield. "Monet."

"I'm not calling for the reason you're probably thinking. No activity going on tonight, far as I know," Downs said at once.

"Good. I'm not in the fucking mood to go fling bullets after the six hours I just put in behind the screen on Moreno. That's why you're calling, isn't it?"

"There's something more to Buenos Aires than what you've sent Homeland. They're looking at the details closely. They think Moreno is more of a direct tie than just providing intelligence."

"What do I need to do?"

"Dig into every link he's got."

"Been doing that already, sir, but I'll double check every word later on. Right now I'm headed out to see a friend."

"Yeah, a break is in order for you. Can't have you losing your shit."

"Thank you, sir." He didn't wait for more, just ended the call. He was finished with Moreno for one night and intended to step as far away from the entire shit-show as possible for a few hours.

Long enough to uncover what was eating at Avery.

The drive to her place didn't take very long, and she buzzed him inside the building. He stared into shadows in each corner of the stairwell, but everything seemed to be quiet and in order. She was safe, and that made him feel a hell of a lot better. If she wasn't with him — in his bed — then at least security measures kept her safe here in her apartment.

She met him at the door with a hug. He pulled her into his embrace and held her close for a long moment.

"It's crazy that it's only been half a day since I saw you and I miss you this much," he said on a whisper.

Her eyes softened. They glimmered in the low light from a lamp in the entryway. "I've been thinking about you too. Come in."

They walked through the apartment, past plants and the sofa piled in cushions. She kept on walking,

145

towing him by the hand, until they reached her bedroom.

His cock hardened at the thought of what she was asking from him—what he was so willing to give. A night in her arms would heal the most broken of men, and he was only a little banged and bruised in spirit.

Following her to the bed, he saw the pillows she'd been propped on when he'd called, a book lying face down on the side table and a lamp on to shed more golden light dancing across her face.

She climbed into bed, legs tucked beneath her in a tight, guarded pose.

With him standing at the bedside, he studied her. "Tell me what happened today that has you knotted up."

She shifted on the mattress, and he sank beside her, close enough to feel her body heat radiating through her lounge pants. Dropping her head, she looked at a loose thread on her comforter and picked at it with a fingertip.

"I paid a visit to the chief today. I guess I didn't hear what I hoped to, and it's been bugging me all day."

"Why didn't you say something earlier when we talked?" After her kickboxing class, he'd called to tell her he had to forego their dinner date in order to work. She had told him she understood—and he knew she did—but she hadn't mentioned her meeting with the chief.

She raised a shoulder and let it fall. "I'm frustrated with all of it, Jess. I feel like I'm running in circles, not getting a bit closer to what I need from the review."

"Your badge back."

She nodded.

He scooted closer and placed a hand over hers, stilling it from picking at the thread. He stared into her eyes. "You know… you don't have to do this all alone, Avery. I'm here to listen. You can confide or rage or just puzzle shit out with me. I'll help you any way I can."

She twisted her hand up to thread their fingers together. "Are you going to tell me about your last six hours sitting at your monitors and listening in on phone calls? Because I can see the slump in your shoulders. And the tension too. C'mere." She inched closer and he moved in as well. When she clamped her hands on his shoulders and kneaded at his stiff muscles, he groaned in pleasure.

He collapsed forward, head against her breasts as she worked over his knotted muscles. "We've both got stressful jobs."

She snorted. "Right now, my biggest stress is the girls in the kickboxing class getting chatty with me and asking me to go for coffee like we're BFFs."

He chuckled softly. "Not your thing?"

"No. Is it odd to admit most of my friends are men?"

"Not at all. Occupational hazard."

"You could say that." She worked along one particularly sore muscle, and he let out a long breath as he felt himself begin to relax.

"So the chief didn't have good news."

"No. He told me to go for anger management classes."

Jess looked up. "Been through a few rounds of those myself. But knowing you, I don't think that's an issue in your life."

"I'm a little offended by the recommendation, to be honest. It makes it seem like I'm out of control and that's why I shot that criminal."

He brushed his lips across the crease in her forehead. "I know that's not true. Many of us know it."

She stopped massaging his shoulders and lifted one hand to cup his jaw. The sensation tore him up with newfound tenderness, something he knew little about but had always sought.

In that moment, he realized that everything he'd hoped to find with those other women from his past, he had finally found when he'd given up searching for it.

He'd found it in Avery.

Love.

Slipping his hand around her nape, he pulled her in. As soon as their lips met, she issued a hungry groan, as if she'd been waiting for this all night. As though it was the only thing she needed in the world.

Desire flashed through him like a blast of C-4. His cock strained against his fly, and he deepened the kiss. Tongues working, they threw themselves together. She locked her arms around his neck and dragged herself close enough that her breasts brushed his chest.

He hauled her across his lap. Her round bottom settled over his thighs, and her eyes widened at what she felt there.

"Take me, Jess. I need to feel..." She broke off, glancing down.

He nudged her face up and pinned her in his stare. "To feel what?" he rasped out.

"Desired."

He made a noise deep in his chest and moved to strip her of the tank top and lounge pants. When he had her stretched out on her bed in only a skimpy pair of cotton panties, he groaned and rubbed a hand over his face.

"Jesus, your panties are soaked. Spread your legs and let me look at you. Yeah, just like that. Fucking hell, baby." He tore at his clothes and had a condom in place in seconds, all while keeping his gaze fixed on the damp spot between her thighs.

Naked and with his cock jutting out, he covered her with his body. She curled around him and found his lips, delivering kisses that grew in intensity. When

149

he eased his fingers over the wet spot on her panties, he bit off the words that had been threatening to loosen his vocal cords since he'd walked through her front door.

I love you. I fucking love you.

He held it back and instead pressed on the crotch of her panties. The cloth gave way and sank between her aroused, pouty lips.

Call him perverted, but he had to look at her, commit the erotic sight to memory. Leaning back on his knees, he parted her thighs and gazed at the cotton worked into her folds.

She shoved on his shoulders, guiding him down, and there wasn't any other place he'd rather be than right here in Avery's bed—between her legs in the heaven of all heavens.

* * * * *

With a gym bag slung over one shoulder and an energizing celery juice in hand, Avery meandered down the sidewalk toward home. Her body felt great. Her heart too, when she allowed her mind to linger over Jess's lovemaking. How he'd stared into her eyes, as if looking into her soul as he thrust his cock into her.

She had far too much time to contemplate what that look in his eyes meant. It was almost as though he… loved her.

She'd never seen love in a man's eyes. Heard the words fall from many men's lips, sure, but she'd known at the time they didn't mean it.

Ugh, she was overthinking again. She needed to let things happen as they were supposed to and shut off her mind when it came to Jess.

The next hour was spent in the psychologist's office and then ten more minutes to set up a time for the anger management classes. Feeling wrung out again, she headed home.

When her phone buzzed, she fished it out of her pocket and saw it was her parents. If she answered, she'd be met with their chipper voices on speakerphone for their weekly call.

Something told her to ignore the call and wait for a better time. She was just stuffing the cell back into her pocket, when it rang a second time.

Fear took hold—her father was sick. Her mom was in the hospital. There'd been an accident.

She pressed it to her ear. "Mom? Dad? I'm here."

"Thanks for the greeting, Aarons." Reggie's low drawl filled her ear, and she felt herself melt with relief.

"Hi, Reg. My parents just called and then I got another one directly after and jumped to conclusions, thinking something might be wrong."

"Not wrong—right. Chief asked me to give you a call. The board wants to meet with you at three."

"Three? Oh God, what time is it?" She'd lost all track between kickboxing, standing in line at the raw juice bar and the appointment with the shrink.

"It's only a little after one. You've got time, Avery. Don't stress. Look, don't get your hopes up either. This might just be more questioning."

Her heart sank from the small place it had lifted to when Reggie told her the board wanted to meet with her.

"All right. I'll keep a level head."

"Yeah, and don't lose your temper with them either."

"What is it you're not telling me? You know something." She narrowed her eyes, not even seeing the sidewalk before her.

"Honest to God, I know as much as you do. But I also know you and how frustrated you've been. Just don't let that get the best of you—I need my partner back."

"I'm always professional."

"Good girl. Call me after the meeting breaks up, okay?"

"I will."

They ended the call, and she gazed at the ribbon of gray cement leading her home to shower and change and then go into the precinct for that meeting.

Reggie's tone of warning reverberated through her head. She didn't know what to think of it. He wouldn't lie to her, not about something as important as her badge. He really must not know what the meeting would be about. Yet... Reggie had the best sixth sense she knew.

And she didn't like his warning one bit.

The remainder of her walk home had her mind clouding with what-ifs. What if she never got her badge back? What if her career was finished? What would she do with her life then?

It sure wasn't teaching kickboxing classes twice a day. She'd be bored out of her mind, bouncing around to the same routine day in and out. Besides, the instructor would return soon.

Maybe her fate wasn't to die at the hands of a criminal—it was to lose the job she loved. Each step home was weighted.

Arriving a good half hour early for the meeting gave her time to hang out in the precinct and get a read on the atmosphere. She sat and talked for a while with the receptionist. Then she and one of the dispatchers, Sadie, shared a coffee. Not much was said to her about the meeting, and Avery was left to read between the lines.

She crossed her legs and brought her coffee cup to her lips and then set it aside again. "I'm already tripping on that caffeine. Better not drink anymore."

Sadie was not someone Avery would call a best friend, but she and Avery hung out together at office Christmas parties or barbecues. When they all hit the cop bar down the street for drinks after a long day, she and Avery would pull up a stool beside each other and shoot the breeze while sipping tequila sunrises.

Sadie looked her over. "You look different."

Oh boy, not her too. Reggie had said something similar days before.

Avery stood and did a three-sixty, showing off her body that had never been so toned. "Twice daily kickboxing."

"Wow, your ass looks great!"

She spun to face Sadie again, laughing. "Boredom sent me to the gym more often."

"You're lucky. Boredom would have sent me to the bakery more often." She stood too, twisting to wiggle her own ass.

They shared a laugh, and for a moment, Avery was grateful for the comic relief. She was so knotted up over what was about to come. The board could drop the guillotine on her days as a cop, and she didn't know what she'd do if that happened.

Seeing this pass over Avery's face, Sadie reached over and patted her hand. "It's going to be okay."

She lifted her brows. "You think so?"

Offering a small smile, Sadie nodded.

At the sound of the chief's voice, she bolted to her feet. He dashed a look at her on the way to his office and said, "Aarons, follow me."

She tossed a glance at Sadie. Her warm smile was meant to reassure, but Avery couldn't help but think it was one of pity.

As she entered the conference room behind Chief Gilbert, she remembered to breathe. Her chest burned with worry. Right now, she wished she could talk to Jess and gain his take on things. But he was off, had been called out in the wee hours of the morning. Their last exchange had been him leaning over her, lips brushing across her forehead. And Avery had clutched his shirt and pulled him down for a real kiss.

Then she'd lain awake for hours after he'd left the condo, worrying if he would be injured this time. Or worse, if she would ever see him again.

If there was one thing she knew, it was that life was short. Maybe her traumas in youth had helped wake her up to that fact, but she never missed out on opportunities to let those around her know they were important.

As a couple gentlemen entered the conference room, she looked up, thoughts of Jess floating away and reality setting in. She greeted them with silent nods. More men entered, and she was relieved to see two ladies were sitting on the review board as well. When the table filled up, she took her chair and rested her hands on the tabletop in a calm manner.

The chief of police looked from person to person. "Let's get started, shall we?"

As the formalities were observed, with the case presented again, and the reports on what had happened in the parking lot that night what felt like ages ago read aloud, Avery fought back the urge to jump up and give her side of the story all over again.

Though, how many times had she stated facts? There was nothing left to say on the matter.

The only question remaining was whether or not they believed she had acted in self-defense or her past had finally caught up to her and she had gone mad.

She listened to the discussion between those in the room.

"...out of her jurisdiction."

"Off duty on top of that..."

"Past psych evals show..."

She did not add to it—after all, she was observing her Miranda rights. She did not wish to make things worse, and at some point, she feared she'd finally lose her temper and it would be all over for her.

"It was recommended that Officer Aarons go through a basic course on anger management." Chief Gilbert turned his head to look at her. "Aarons, have you done so?"

"I've enrolled, sir. The course doesn't begin until this Friday."

"All right, then. We give Officer Aarons time to complete the course and then reconvene here the following week. Is that acceptable to everybody?" He glanced around at the other members of the review session.

Nods answered him, and then the meeting was finished. She stared in shock as people left the room.

She got to her feet. "Nothing changed. Nothing happened. Why was a meeting even held today?" she asked the chief.

He eyed her. "Avery, these things take time and we require that every channel be investigated. You can't rush it." He gave her a stern look. "Not even by having your friend call and demand answers."

She blinked at him. "Excuse me?"

"This morning, a former Texas Ranger by the name of Jess Monet called asking about your case. He was warned to back off, and I'll reiterate that sentiment with you right now, Officer Aarons."

Her heart jerked against her chest wall so hard that it knocked the breath from her. She could do nothing but stare at the chief for a long moment. Finally, words flooded onto her tongue.

"I assure you that I had nothing to do with that. If Jess did call, then it was his own idea."

"That may be true, but it doesn't look good for you. Lucky for you, I did not share that information here today. Now, I've got work to do. You know the way out."

Dismissed, she gathered herself up and left the precinct. Her mind was cluttered, fogged with everything that had taken place. And just what had Jess been thinking to call and interfere? This was her life—and a man she'd been seeing all of ten minutes wasn't going to jeopardize her position.

Anger washed over her, hot and brighter than the Texas sun blasting down on her head. Each step she took toward the parking garage where her car was made her burn more with fury.

Trouble was, she couldn't even direct it at Jess. He was off doing God knew what to protect their country from threats.

The tough guy thought he could fix everything, but that wasn't the case here, and he'd only complicated things for her.

Chapter Eight

"Jess, we need you on this." Colonel Downs held out a sheet of paper to him.

He shot the colonel a look before taking the paper from his hand. One glance, and he knew exactly who they'd intercepted the message from.

"I'm on it." He was already moving to the conference table and sinking to a chair, his eyes locked on the words of the message. "How was this received? Email?"

"Text from Moreno to Acosta."

Jess nodded absently, his brain shooting ahead to which letters were to be replaced by others, therefore shaking the entire message up like a box of Scrabble game pieces and revealing a message with another meaning.

He plucked a pen from his pocket and began scribbling under the words. He murmured under his breath as he worked. The colonel stood back, arms folded, and watched him a minute.

Jess looked up. "I'll get this to you as soon as I'm finished."

He nodded and walked out of the room, leaving Jess alone with a cloud of letters and ciphers in his mind.

He stared at one letter in particular. At a glance, he knew it'd been used twelve times within the message, and that wasn't only coincidence.

Replacing it with letters wasn't getting him anywhere, and he drew a breath and started over again.

As soon as one word clicked into place, he clenched a fist on his knee. "Colonel Downs!"

The man must have been standing just outside the door, because he stepped into the room in a second. "What is it?"

"A strike."

"Where?"

"I'm about to..." He fell silent as another word locked in.

He looked up at Downs.

"Location?"

"Puerto Madryn."

"You're certain of this?"

"A hundred percent. But there's more. I..." He drifted off again, lost in the letters that wouldn't mean anything to a person who didn't know Moreno as a man. A man who was paid for trading espionage, who would replace the twelfth letter of the alphabet with the first letter of his daughter's name. Every L in

160

the message—all twelve of them—were replaced with Ms, the first letter of his late wife's name.

He jolted in his seat. "Oh God."

"What is it?" Colonel Downs leaned over the table, an expectant expression on his hard features.

"The twelfth is the date the attack will occur, and that's—"

"Tomorrow," Downs finished. He spun to the door and bellowed for Sully. Their captain's thumping footsteps echoed in the hallway and their voices reached Jess.

"I'm dispatching troops to Puerto Madryn. Ready your team. You and Knight Ops are heading to Chiapas to go after Moreno as soon as I can get a helo here."

Jess got to his feet. "Colonel."

The officer stared at him.

"Moreno cannot thwart an attack—he's just the middle man, handing off the baton from one to another. Even if we take him into custody, it's unlikely an attack can be stopped. It's been in place for weeks now—months even, and there will already be men on the ground in Puerto Madryn."

Downs gave a stiff nod. "We're aware these men don't follow him, Monet. But he's the pivot point in all these attacks, and we have to suspect him as one who could be calling the shots and not only delivering the intelligence as we first believed. Anything else?"

Jess nodded. "His children live with him, sir. If we attack his home, it's likely we will kill innocent children."

"Then we'll have to do our best not to let that happen. Sully, your team."

"On it, sir."

Jess dropped back to his seat, sweating, heart racing.

It was finally happening — all his late nights spent listening to phone calls and deciphering correspondence between Moreno and countless men was finally coming to a head.

They were set to attack Moreno in his own home.

Even if the Ranger Ops saved Moreno's son and daughter, by dawn of the next day, their father would be dead and the children orphans.

He planted his elbows on the table and jammed his fingers through his hair. "Fuck."

* * * * *

On a map, seeing Moreno's big house and plot of land his family had owned since back in the days of coffee farming was one thing. Seeing it in person was quite another.

He stared at the rich beauty of the landscape before him. The white stucco house with the clay red roof was nestled up against a backdrop of what looked like rainforest. But Jess knew just on the other side of those trees was a small town where Moreno took his kids for treats like ice creams and *torta de tres leches.*

He swallowed hard enough he heard it in his own ears. On his three, Cav peered through his rifle scope at the windows of the house.

"We need him to come to one of the windows and it's all over," Cav said, low.

"Just make fucking sure one of the kids isn't around."

"I'm aware of the situation, Jess. Just take it easy, okay?" Cav didn't look away from the window that was trimmed in the same red as the tiled roof. The yard was a series of terraced gardens with barriers of hedgerows that created an octagonal pattern across the property. In the center of everything sat a small gazebo with a thatched roof, and Jess could easily picture the children going there to play or relax after finishing their schoolwork.

Cav jerked, his finger perched on the trigger. Jess pressed his own eye to the scope but saw nothing in the window. From the bottom corner of his vision, he tracked movement.

"A dog," Woody said into their comms unit.

"No, a goat," Jess responded. "The goat's name is Vincent Van Goat."

A chuckle sounded to his right, and Cav moved his rifle away from the harmless animal.

"Why the hell did they name a goat?" Cav asked.

"It's the kids' pet."

"I got movement, and it's not the four-legged variety." Sully's drawl had Jess's adrenaline kicking in big time.

His heart slammed faster, and he positioned himself as backup to the shot Woody, as sharpshooter, was set up to take.

"Jess, we need confirmation. Top right window. Is that our guy?"

He lowered his rifle and peered through high-power binoculars. As soon as he saw the outline of the man, he thought it might be. But then he snapped his jaw shut as the face came into focus.

"No, that's the caretaker."

"What's he doing in the house? Does he stay inside it?"

"No... he's got a small hut behind the structure. He must be..." Realization struck.

"Fuck!" Jess's cuss had Cav pivoting to look at him.

Jess went on, "The only reason the caretaker would be in the house is he's checking on things— because the family's not home. Otherwise, he only goes into Moreno's office to speak to him about issues."

"Dammit." This came from Sully. "Woody, hold your position. Jess, take the others and go internal. But watch for the old man. He'll be prepared to defend the place."

Jess got into a crouch and waved the others forward.

Going into the home he knew as well as he knew the house he'd grown up in with his mom and three brothers felt surreal. As he passed by a bicycle parked on the veranda, his stomach twisted. It was Moreno's son's bike, a gift from his *papa* for his ninth birthday.

"Shit," he said under his breath and continued on.

He had to keep his head in the game. He knew what had to happen.

An hour later, they walked out of Chiapas and boarded their transport once again, the mission complete and a total dead end. The frightened caretaker knew nothing of where Moreno had taken his family, only that he would return in three days' time.

One thing was certain — they'd made themselves known to Moreno by approaching that caretaker. He'd be on to them and most likely bury himself further underground with the dregs of humanity he dealt with.

Jess didn't know whether to feel relieved that it hadn't ended in a bloodbath or if he was pissed that Moreno was still out there, a crucial link to countless attacks spanning the years.

What was it that drove Moreno to trade dark intel? It had to be the money. Greed was a huge driving factor for most. It had provided him with the funds to update the land he'd inherited and keep his family home from becoming rundown and swallowed by the forest. It afforded him men to watch over his house and clip his hedges. It bought his children nice things.

But Jess had an inkling money wasn't the only factor—which meant it must be power. Moreno had made himself important. He only had to give his name and people accepted his calls immediately.

Cav shifted next to Jess. "Damn, I wish it'd been him in the window. One twitch of Woody's finger, and it would all be over. These guys who rely on Moreno would be scrambling without him."

"Yeah, all over." Jess stared at his hands, which were clean of blood... as was his conscience, at least when it came to Moreno's kids. Today they still had a father. But not for very fucking long.

* * * * *

For two days, Avery had wondered what to say to Jess when she saw him again, and each time her mind toiled over the possibilities, it came up blank in the end.

Now she had about ten minutes to figure it out. If her anger management class had taught her anything on the first day, it was to think of the outcomes of her words and actions.

But deep down, she was furious that Jess had interfered in her work life. He had no right even if

166

they hadn't been going out for such a short time and —

There she went again, letting angry words fill her brain, when she needed to consider some that wouldn't end her relationship with the only man who'd ever been important to her, along with her career in law enforcement crashing and burning.

She scooted to the edge of her sofa and dropped her face into her hands, breathing slow and deep.

When the buzzer sounded, she lifted her head and stared at the security camera trained on the door.

She tried to keep her damn heart from leaping in her chest, but it did anyway.

The camera was angled downward over the man who stood waiting for her to let him into the building, giving her a view of his bowed head and broad shoulders.

Shit—some of her anger was fading away now that she got a good look at her lover. A man shouldn't be able to strip away her emotions so easily—or instill them either. Yet just looking at him, she couldn't stop the thrum of her heart and the emotions building for him.

If she was honest with herself, she couldn't deny those fluttery feelings could be more. They could be…

He poked the buzzer again, and she moved to let him in. A minute later, he stood at her door, looking down on her with that crooked smile cutting a path over his rugged features.

Damn him. Why did he have to look at her like that?

He reached for her, and she remembered the problem he'd made for her when he'd taken it upon himself to call the chief.

She took a step back. Confusion lit his eyes, and he closed the door quietly behind him.

Studying her closely, he kept his distance, which was good, because she didn't quite know how to deal with him.

"Avery. What happened?"

"Jess, don't pretend you don't know. You happened. You called the chief and asked about my review. Why?" Settling a hand on her hip, she eyed him.

He let his gaze skip away from hers and turned it up to the ceiling for a moment. When he met her glare again, his eyes were soft with emotion but his lips were set into a fine line.

He didn't answer.

She stepped up to him, so close she caught a whiff of his masculine body wash. That only set her mind spinning again with the knowledge that he'd probably just climbed out of a chopper and rushed through a shower, in a hurry to see her.

The knowledge didn't stop her from being angry at him for the situation.

"Why, Jess? You made me look like a fool, like I can't take care of myself."

"Shit, that isn't what I wanted. Avery —"

"Well, it's what happened. And my chief told me you needed to back off, as if I'd set you on my case. My career's already in the toilet, and you tried to flush it on me!"

"No, I didn't. Avery, I just wanted to help. You've done so much for me. I just wanted to return the favor for you helping me with Madison, and all that work you did on the family tree when I was gone last time."

She waved a hand in dismissal. "You can't just barge into people's lives and take over, even if that's what you do as an operative."

"That's not what I was trying to do. Dammit, baby, listen. I wanted to help."

She released a low laugh. "You didn't help, Jess. And I'm capable of handling it myself."

"I know you are, but dammit —"

"Dammit, what? You wanted to take over, throw around your name and rank?"

"No. Goddammit. I'm a born protector. And I was trying to save you from losing the job you fucking love. Is that enough reason for you? Because it's more than enough for me that I tried to help out the woman *I* love —"

Her jaw dropped. She froze in place, all words tipping out of her mind.

He went on.

"I thought a call to the chief might speed things along, let them know that it wasn't okay to be stringing you on all these weeks." He caught her stare. "Say something." He pitched his voice low. "You're gutting me here, baby."

"You..." The words died on her lips. She tried again. "You just said you love me." .

He blinked a few times as if it was news to him as well. Maybe it was just words, spat in the heat of the moment. Maybe—

He stepped up to her and rested a hand along her cheek. "Fuck it. I've spent years trying to back away from women, and you're the only one my gut is telling me to run toward instead. I'm in love with you, baby, and I have been since the first time I saw you in that CPR class."

A sound broke from her throat. She leaned into his hand and closed her eyes, letting the words and moment sink in.

When she opened her eyes again, she saw fear tinting the depths of Jess's eyes, darkening them.

He leaned closer. "If you're kicking me out of your life, do it now while I can still walk away. I'd hate to crawl out of here."

"Jess. I was upset that you brought my chief down on me for your call."

"I understand. I shouldn't have done it."

"You were trying to help, I see that now. I'm sorry I got so angry with you when you were only trying to help me."

He caressed her cheek with his thumb. "I'd say I won't try to watch over you again, unless you tell me you don't feel anything for me too."

She released a breath. "I can't believe a man in your position wouldn't already know the answer to that. You must have been aware that I've been throwing myself at you since the CPR class. I wanted you to ask me out, and you were friend-zoning me instead. And when you go away, I can barely breathe thinking of something happening to you and wondering when I'll see you again."

A smile ghosted across his face. "Then I do something to make you mad."

"Now that I know where you were coming from, I'm not mad. And you know what you said about loving me?"

He nodded.

"I feel the very same," she whispered.

He closed his eyes briefly and then opened them. The fear was gone, replaced by joy.

Without another word, he caught her in his arms and crushed his lips over hers.

* * * * *

Avery removed a paperclip from a stack of printouts and spread them over her kitchen counter.

171

Jess leaned over her shoulder, hands on her waist, and read over what she'd found.

Releasing her, he picked up a sheet. "You went back into 18th century England to find my father's great-grandmother?"

She nodded, her hair soft against his cheek.

"All of this for my daughter?"

"Well, for you too." She twisted to look up at him.

He stared into her eyes a moment before he was drawn back to the papers. "You're freakin' amazing. Have I told you that lately?"

"Not in the past half hour."

"Well, let me say it now." With a swipe, he cleared the papers from the counter and lifted her onto it. Wedging himself between her legs, he took her face in his hands and kissed her.

Quickly, it spiraled from a caress to bold exploration and need. When she wrapped her thighs around him, he lifted her and turned, thinking of laying her down on the closest soft piece of furniture. But they didn't make it to the sofa or bed — he laid her down on the kitchen floor.

She tore at his shirt and ran her hands over his muscles. He ripped hers overhead and cupped one breast while reaching for her bra clasp.

She threw her head back on a laugh as he sprang it free, but the sound cut off abruptly as he sucked her nipple into his mouth.

Within moments they were both stripped and Avery had a condom in hand, a twinkle in her eyes.

"Let's get this on you, babe." A wicked grin spread over her beautiful face.

When she slid it over his hard cock with torturous movements of her hand, he closed his eyes, fighting for control. She took over more by rolling out from under him and straddling his hips.

Fuck, looking up at her, powerful, beautiful and sexy as hell, was going to kill him. He couldn't wait another minute. Grabbing her hips, he lifted her over his cock.

She settled hard and fast, taking him to the hilt.

As a groan hit his throat, a cry of pleasure echoed off her kitchen walls. Need spanned him, locking down his need to give Avery the most intense pleasure of her life.

She rocked over him, and they shared another moan. When she started to move faster, he caught one hip in his hand and the other pressed against her cheek. Looking into her eyes, he grated out, "Slow, baby."

She stilled, the hunger warring in her eyes with a flicker of love. Slowly, she leaned over him, breasts to chest, their gazes catching. When they moved again, it was subtle movements that somehow seemed to amp everything even higher.

His cock squeezed precum from the tip, and she clenched and released around him with each downward glide. When their mouths met, it was a sweet bonding, a melding he never believed could be real. He knew all those who'd come before her were nothing to him.

Passion rose up, and she kissed him with everything she had, pulling more from him.

"Fuck, I love you," he rasped.

"Love you too." She sucked on his lower lip, raising a growl from him. Balls aching, he took her ass in his hands and worked her over him faster. The heat took over, and soon they were slamming to the finish line. As Avery called out his name, he held her stare. It was all over for him—he was never letting this woman go.

* * * * *

Headquarters was all silent, the other Ranger Ops long gone. All but Jess. Instead of wasting time going home, he'd gotten caught in the web of Moreno and what OFFSUS believed to be time-sensitive intelligence.

Taking it had meant calling Madison and pushing back their time to meet at the coffeeshop later this evening.

At his elbow, he also had a hefty sheaf of printouts on his own family history, some Avery had done on her own, some they'd completed together, and much he'd uncovered on his own hunt. He had everything organized into a spreadsheet for Madison to complete her family tree project.

If Moreno ever wrapped up this bullshit conversation, Jess could get the hell out of here. From what Jess could decipher it wasn't anything important—just soccer highlights. But he guessed even terrorist masterminds needed hobbies too.

For a moment, he listened to the scores repeated and compared them to the ones posted on the sports page. All checked out, down to the digit. Nothing out of line here.

He adjusted his earpiece to listen more closely to the talk, translating the Spanish seamlessly and typing it into the system. He hadn't learned a thing about Moreno's reason for fleeing his home that day the Ranger Ops invaded. They all suspected something had tipped the man off, forced him to take his kids and run.

But he hadn't yet returned to the house in Chiapas either. They'd traced his calls to Mexico City, closer to the attacks popping up all over the country. Each time they believed they had him cornered, Moreno would slip away. But finding him would lead them to many of the terrorist cells plaguing so many countries and even the US.

Jess was feeling the pressure too. Damn if they were losing this asshole again—this time, he was determined to hear *something* that put them in Moreno's path.

The intel spread across the computer monitors would make a spy pant with desire. Jess had Moreno's life on screen, as well as every person connected to him, many responsible for atrocities on humanity that would earn them the death penalty.

Which they would receive, if OFFSUS had anything to do with it.

He leaned back in his chair and closed his eyes a moment, listening to their conversation.

A hand clamped onto his shoulder, and he jerked upright to see Sully standing over him.

"Shit, man, you could warn a guy before you sneak up on him." Jess eyed his captain.

Sully leaned against the long table and folded his arms. "I thought you'd be long gone. What made you stay here to work instead of going home?"

"The call came in before I could leave. Figured I'd better not miss anything."

"You could have handed it off to another operative," he said, referring to those team members of OFFSUS who worked behind the scenes on intel.

"I wanted to hear for myself."

Sully stared at him, unblinking.

Jess huffed out a sigh. "Just say it, man. I know there's something on your mind."

Sully dropped his arms and gripped onto the edge of the table. "Okay. I think you're too fucking close to this and you need a break."

176

"You'd better mean take a break like go home and eat a pizza."

"Not exactly."

Jess slowly got to his feet and faced his captain. "Are you sidelining me?"

"It would only be on the Moreno stuff."

"Hell no." Jess's raised voice echoed throughout the room.

Sully pulled away from the tables, and they faced off.

Jess took a step closer to the man—his friend and superior—but Jess wasn't against telling the great Nash Sullivan he was wrong on this matter.

"I'm not backing off this case. I'm the one who got us to Chiapas, remember? We were *this* close to nabbing him."

Sully arched a brow. "You were very concerned with Moreno's children."

"What's that got to do with anything? Of course I don't want to be responsible for a hit on kids." His tone escalated once more, his anger banking fast.

"Colonel Downs and I—"

"Wait—this is coming from higher up? You spoke with Downs about it before bringing it to me? You didn't give me a chance to state my side, did you? Son of a bitch!" He turned and strode away from Sully, crossing the room where he had distance between them, and time to decide if he should punch his captain's teeth in.

"We've discussed it before, Jess. You were told to get a handle on your stress levels with this case in particular. Since you haven't—"

"How the hell do you know whether or not I'm stressed?" Jess exploded. "I've never made a single error as an operative. Never have I failed to perform."

"That's true, but I'm also trained to spot warning signs in my men."

He barked out a harsh laugh. "What are you 'spotting' then? Go on and tell me." He clenched his hands at his sides.

"Restlessness, fatigue. You're not sleeping."

"Maybe that's because I have a girlfriend I'm up all night fucking," he shot out. "Remember those days with your own wife, man?"

"That's not it, Jess. Admit it."

"I refuse to admit something I don't believe is true. My only problem with this case is that I don't want to see Moreno's kids harmed. I've got my own daughter to think about here—"

"Ahh, now we're getting to the root of this."

Jess crossed the room so fast he didn't remember anything but the thuds of his boots on the floor as he closed the distance between them. An inch from Sully's face, he burst out, "You think because you found out that I'm a father that you can say I'm allowing my personal views to blur what's going on with a terrorist spy? Dude, that's like saying since you had your kid that you're unfit to lead because a child might be involved."

All the heat and fury threatened to explode from his body. He stepped back to keep himself from knocking Sully on his fucking ass.

"Stand down, Monet. We're just having a conversation, nothing more."

"No? Seems like an accusation to me. You're telling me I'm unfit because of my personal life getting in the way."

All of a sudden, realization smacked him.

Avery.

She was in the same damn boat with her review and her history… and neither of them had a damn paddle in sight.

Except he wasn't going to allow his captain to strip responsibility from him the way it had been forced on Avery.

Fuck.

He glared at Sully. "I'm putting this to bed. I'm going to find Moreno and we're going in to kill him. How's that for personal? I'm going to call down the strike that will orphan his children, but it's for the good of mankind. Now leave me alone so I can do my job."

The finality of his words rendered Sully silent. He stood there a moment watching Jess. "I've got orders too, man. Don't forget who tells me what to do."

"Yeah, Colonel Downs, OFFSUS, the fucking Pentagon, whatever." It didn't make it any better for Jess.

Sully went out. Jess listened to his footsteps travel down the hall to his own office, where he'd probably put in a call to Colonel Downs.

Picking up his headset once more, he settled before the computer system. Dead air met his ears— Moreno's conversation was over, picked up by his backup in another office in some other city, and Jess had missed it.

He pushed out a frustrated sigh and stared at what he'd recorded today. Not enough to get the asshole.

Shoving a hand through his hair, he turned his attention to written correspondence.

Maybe it was the adrenaline running through his veins from his argument with Sully. But suddenly, he read between the lines.

Something totally different stuck out to him.

Moreno... he'd been in the US not even a week ago.

"Fuck." He got Colonel Downs on the phone and filled him in—Moreno was coming in through underground channels, and the thought he could be scoping things out for a bigger target had Downs and the entirety of Homeland Security on red alert.

Another hour and a half later, Jess was finally dismissed for the night, and hanging up that headset felt damn good. It also felt like he'd just given Downs and Sully the middle finger. And they thought he was too close to make calls on Moreno?

Despite his victory today, Jess rubbed the bridge of his nose, trying to alleviate the headache spreading behind his eyes.

Poor Avery. She'd been dealing with the same bullshit from her precinct. Jess probably hadn't been supportive enough to her. The same way OFFSUS was accusing Jess of not getting Moreno because they'd just discovered he was a father was the same as Avery being told her past had caused her to shoot that man in the parking lot.

He regretted trying to speak to the police chief to help her. If the roles were reversed, he wouldn't have welcomed her intrusion either, and he deserved every angry word she'd spouted off at him. He was also damn lucky she'd understood his side and forgiven him.

He checked his watch and registered the time. Right now, she was wrapping up one of the kickboxing classes she was so fond of but he knew was also keeping her mind off her problems with the review. After her workout, she was heading to the mandatory anger management class they had forced on her. Meanwhile, he was meeting Madison at the coffeeshop, and then he and Avery were joining up for a late dinner.

He spent a few minutes leafing through the papers he had for his daughter and waiting for

Moreno to make another call. After twenty minutes or so, he gave up and left the headquarters.

The parking lot was empty—Sully had taken off as well. Jess's anger with his captain had dissipated. Maybe it was true Sully was seeing signs of stress in him. Maybe he didn't even recognize it in himself.

With yet another heavy topic to chew on, Jess drove to the coffeeshop where he'd been with Avery that day Madison had made the overture to approach him. His heart still leaped with warmth when he thought of that day, and the phone calls and texts he and his daughter had shared since then only added to his feeling that he might be on the right track with her.

At last.

When he reached the coffeeshop, he entered to see Madison and her mom seated at a table near the front so he could easily pick them out of the crowd. He meandered through tables to reach them.

Jenna stood. "Madison says she'd like to spend some time with you alone going over the project. I'm going to run some errands, and I'll come back for her."

His gaze flicked from Jenna to his daughter. A faint pink flush crested her cheekbones, and his heart tugged at the thought she could be nervous with him. He had news for her too—he was equally as nervous.

"Why don't I just bring her home when we finish up?" he asked Jenna.

She looked around at Madison, who gave a tiny nod. She directed her attention to Jess again. "That will be fine."

"I'll have her text you before we leave so you'll know we're on our way."

"I'd appreciate that. Thanks, Jess."

His throat closed off momentarily. He cleared it. "Thanks for this. For… everything. Most of all, for giving me the chance I probably don't deserve."

Jenna placed a hand on his forearm and squeezed before letting go. "It's never too late. Have fun," she called out with a wave to their daughter.

Jess transferred the file of papers he had to under one arm. "Wanna grab some of those cinnamon rolls they have here?" he asked Madison.

She nodded and got up. He placed a hand on her back to steer her to the counter, where they ordered snacks and drinks. Then they sat at the best seat in the house next to the window and people-watched for a while before Jess opened the folder and they started on the project.

With a stomach full of treats and a warm heart, Jess drove her home. There, he received a genuine hug from Madison. Holding her in his arms brought tears to his eyes. But when she went on tiptoe to kiss his cheek, one of the tears escaped the corner of his eye and rolled down his cheek.

He brushed it away when she stepped back. She rubbed at her lips. "You need a shave."

He chuckled, lifting a hand to his two-day-old stubble. "You're right. Next time I'll be sure to do that. Bye, princess. Let me know how the project goes. I'd like to see it when you're finished with the family tree."

"I'll text ya."

He grinned. "I'll be waiting."

He watched her walk into her house and heard a faint call of "Mom, I'm home!" before he walked back to his car and climbed behind the wheel.

As soon as he was alone again, his thoughts turned darker, Moreno weighting him down again.

Dammit—maybe he really did have a problem with stress.

Chapter Nine

Avery lifted a slice of pepperoni and mushroom pizza to her lips, her eyes on Jess rather than the movie they'd put on for their evening's entertainment.

Something was wrong—he was silent and withdrawn, that much was evident. But she couldn't help but feel there was more going on in that brain of his.

Was it Madison? Avery knew he'd met with her earlier at the coffeeshop to exchange details about the project. But maybe something had happened he hadn't told Avery about. When asked about the date with his daughter, he'd only mumbled that it went well.

After watching him devour a slice of pizza so fast that she wondered if he was tasting it at all or just on autopilot, she set aside her own slice. Just as she was about to open her mouth and ask what was putting him into this mood, his phone buzzed.

His gaze slid to hers. He swiped his lips with a napkin and got to his feet, unfolding to his full height and making her crane her neck to see him.

"Monet," he bit off, starting out of the room for privacy.

Avery sighed and reached for her pizza again. Her body was telling her after kickboxing that it needed fuel, but she'd lost her appetite with worry.

A moment later, he strode back into the room. From six feet away, he looked at her, jaw clenched.

"This is it. I have to go."

She stumbled to her feet and crossed the space to him, placing her arms around him. He quivered with tension — or was it something more?

She tilted her head to meet his gaze. "Jess, what is it?"

"Can't say."

"But you're worried."

"Not worried exactly. Just… on edge, I guess."

"Can't you tell me anything so I can help ease you a bit?"

He pushed out a rough breath and gripped her shoulders. "Baby, you're amazing. More than I deserve."

She started to shake her head. "That's not true."

He stopped her. "It is true. I don't deserve to have you."

"Jess, where is this coming from?"

Rather than answer her direct question, he said, "I'm sorry again for trying to get information out of the chief about your review. I shouldn't have — "

She stopped him this time with a forefinger on his lips. "Dammit, you're going to tell me what's going on before you leave here."

"Baby, I've only got a few minutes. The team can't get held up because of me."

"I know that. But just give me some hint as to where you're going and why it's upsetting you so much."

"Fuck." He pulled from her hold and walked a few feet away.

When he looked at her, she saw a burning in his eyes that she'd never seen before. Her heart did a somersault.

"I've been following this guy, gathering intelligence on him. We thought we had him and we went in a couple weeks back."

She nodded, urging him to go on.

"It's as if… It's… Fuck." He jammed his fingers through his hair, ruffling it and standing it on end.

She wanted nothing more than to hug him and soothe him, but she knew men like Jess. No—she knew *Jess*. And he wouldn't appreciate her attempts to comfort when his mind was a locked vault holding in the hard things he had to do for his country's sake.

"Go on," she said quietly.

"The guy's got kids. I've listened to them so much, I feel like I know them. It's more personal, and it's different from the other situations I've been in. The anonymity is gone, and I'm not sure Sully and the others get it—how it makes me feel. But he's also delivering intel into the hands of psycho terrorists. He's shared information about attacks in South America, and there's another planned. Which means we're going in there and killing this motherfucker so we can get to the others before they take out half of Mexico City. But doing so means his kids could be in danger. But either way, I'm taking their father's life." He made a fist and struck his chest. "And that is fucking killing me."

Her throat tightened. "Oh Jess."

He dragged in a breath, staring at her. "I'm okay. I'm going to do it, because it needs done, and the world is better off without this asshole in it."

"You know he's doing this to himself. He's made the choice to leave his children from the minute he got involved in this sort of activity."

"I know. It's like firing yourself for being late to work every day. He's digging his own grave. But what makes all this worse is Sully and Colonel Downs don't believe I'm capable of keeping my distance on this."

"Can you?" she asked.

His face blanked. After a moment, he gave a hard nod. "Yeah, I can."

"Then do it, Jess. Do your job as well as I know — and you know — that you can. But don't leave without knowing this." She rushed to him and threw her arms around his neck. "I love you," she said against his chest, her words muffled.

His arms came around her.

She looked up and lost herself in the depths of his eyes. "Come back to me, Jess Monet."

"I will. Fuck. I love you, Avery." He tipped her face up and leaned in to brush his lips across hers. He tasted of pizza and man and all the things she loved about Jess.

He crushed her against him, and she held on tight. When they broke the kiss, she looked up into his eyes. "You've got this."

"I know." He searched her eyes. "And baby…"

"Yes?"

"So do you. That board is going to come to the realization that they'd be idiots to lose you. And very soon." He cupped her face and planted a kiss between her brows.

He drew away and strode to the door. He threw a wave, and then he was gone.

She sighed out a plume of the emotions whirling through her, and it took her only seconds to realize they were all good. Admitting her love for Jess had somehow freed her more than she'd ever expected. The world felt exciting with new possibilities. She had supportive friends in the precinct and an amazing man who loved her.

Her gaze fell on the coffee table and she spotted yet another possibility—having an entire pizza to herself.

A smile spread across her lips as she fell to the sofa and curled up in the corner with her slice.

* * * * *

"Load up, guys. Chopper's waiting." Sully stood at the door, ushering the Ranger Ops team out to the SUV.

Jess slung his pack over his back and cinched the straps around the waist. Rushing through the procedure of grabbing their gear always made him worry about forgetting something crucial. He'd been the last man in and the last man out the door, and there was little time for wondering if he'd forgotten something. He had to trust that he'd organized everything and it was already in his pack.

As he passed Sully, the man threw out an arm to stop him. Jess looked up.

"Monet, about earlier."

He waited.

"I was out of line. I see all you're doing, and I realize it's impossible to keep your head out of it at times. I've been there. I owe you an apology."

Jess gave him a nod. "We're good, man."

"Glad to hear it. Now get your late ass in that vehicle." He slapped him on the ass as he went by, and Jess chuckled the rest of the way to the SUV.

190

The guys were in a rare mood, laughing and shooting jokes back and forth. It lightened the mood of what they were about to do, and for that, Jess was grateful.

He also caught himself replaying his moments with Avery right before leaving. How she'd stared up at him — sweet, soft, beautiful woman, with her heart glowing all the way into her eyes.

Oh, he'd come back to her, all right. And he'd pick her up and carry her to bed and keep her pinned beneath him, crying out in ecstasy, for the first day or two. After that, he'd take her someplace nice where he could wear a tie and eye up her sexy legs in a pretty dress. Someplace with terrific food to go with the amazing company. Maybe they'd finally get around to that people-watching. Then reminisce over that mouth-to-mouth they'd learned the first time they'd met.

He had so much to celebrate and more to lose than ever before. Avery and Madison both had become priorities in his life in such a short time. How odd to think that mere months ago, he'd been battling loneliness and a measure of depression from keeping his own counsel.

In minutes they reached the airport where the chopper waited. As they ducked under the blades and climbed into the craft, Jess tossed Cav a grin. "Ready, man?" he called out over the din.

"Always fuckin' ready." Cav tossed him a smile of his own as he settled into position along the wall.

They weren't in the air two minutes before the party atmosphere fell away, and each man grew serious. Cav stopped cracking jokes and became quiet. Sully pulled out a photo of his wife and child, looking at it with a half-smile on his face before he slipped it back into his pocket.

The others retreated to their own thoughts, Jess included.

His mind was on Moreno.

The man had to come to justice for his crimes. He wished there was such a thing as rehabilitating some of these guys they hunted. But there wasn't. His momma always told him once a pickle turned bad, it would poison the entire jar and then they all had to be thrown away.

By taking down Moreno, it was possible his children could be saved—they might not yet be poisoned.

"Approaching Mexican airspace," the pilot announced over the intercom.

Sully suddenly snapped his head up and stared at Jess. "Cav, get outta that seat," he barked.

Cav jumped up and moved to take Sully's as their captain landed next to Jess. He thrust his phone into his face.

"What the fuck does this mean?" Sully demanded.

He took the phone from him and gazed at the message there. A message from an unknown person with no traceable number.

"How the hell'd you get this?" he asked.

"It just came through as soon as we dropped altitude."

"Shit." He was looking at what appeared to be a message from a commander or a colonel, but something more stuck out to Jess.

A series of letters at the end, a signature of sorts, but scrambled. Jess knew damn well what they meant.

He jerked his head up to pierce Sully in his stare. "They're onto us. Moreno's calling us out—and it's not here in Mexico."

The guys stared at him.

"It's on our own turf."

* * * * *

"Is there an Avery Aarons in this class?" A woman stood at the door of the gym's classroom, her face tense.

Avery swung her leg down from her high kick and turned at once. "That's me."

"Urgent phone call for you."

She felt the blood drain from her face, down her body and all the way out her toes.

Jess. Something must be wrong with Jess.

193

She pictured him as she'd last seen him, rough and rugged. His face creased with worry and the gold of his cross necklace glinting.

She felt herself move but didn't register she was walking until she reached the woman at the door. Her vision wobbled in and out as she was led to the front counter and handed the phone.

She brought it to her ear. "Avery Aarons here." Her mouth was suddenly chalky.

"Woman, you are a fucking hard one to track down. Are you looking at a TV?" Reggie's voice only confused her further. Was this about Jess?

"No, I was working out."

"There's a huge threat to the city, and it's all hands on deck."

The words sank into her muddled brain. Threat. Here in Austin.

"Bomb threats are going up. We need you, Aarons. Meet me at this address. I'm not going in without my partner at my side."

"Reg—"

"Dammit, you're not hearing me, are you? We fucking need you. We're spread thin all over the city, and we need more uniforms!"

She stared at the dead phone in her hand before dropping it to the desk. She waved at the workers there. "Turn on the news now! Follow whatever instructions they give you and keep everyone here safe!"

She ran for the locker room and changed into her jeans and top in seconds. Running out again, she tried to hail a cab, but they kept zooming by her.

Finally, she jumped in front of one, waving her arms. The driver rolled down the window. "Lady, we've been told there's some major problem here in the city and we're to return to the garage right now."

"Where's your garage?" she shot out.

He named a place.

"Take me that far and I'll give you double the rate."

He nodded, and she jumped into the passenger's seat. Without asking permission, she switched his radio to a news station. The report projecting through the speakers was dour.

The cabby threw her a look. "That doesn't sound good, does it?"

"No, it doesn't. How fast can you drive?"

"Where are you really headed, lady? You got kids at one of those church daycares they're talking about being threatened or something?"

"I'm a cop. I need to reach the Municipal Court building—now!"

"Well then, I can take a detour." He whipped the cab down a side street at a high rate of speed. She quickly reached for her phone. The lines to the precinct were all busy, even Chief Gilbert's direct line.

"Dammit," she swore to herself, ending the call and dialing a new one.

She knew Jess had gone dark since leaving for his mission, so calling him was futile. But she could perhaps save someone he cared about.

"Jenna. It's Avery Aarons. I need you to get Madison and head home as soon as you get this message. Please take any route outside the city limits that you can to get to your house. If you can't get there on other roads, then get out of Austin and drive west. There's a threat to the city—a bunch of them. Please listen to me."

The cab driver threw her a wild look. "Should I even bother going to the garage? I've got my old dad in one of the nursing homes. Maybe I should go get him."

"No. Just listen to your boss and get to the garage. Your dad will be looked after. Okay?"

He nodded and took several narrow streets and alleyways to jet them around the most congested area of the city. When they reached the Municipal Court, bomb squads, SWAT vehicles and police cars were barricading the front. Firetrucks and rescue units were on standby as well.

Avery jumped out and threw a handful of cash at the driver. "Thank you so much! Stay safe!"

"You too!" he called before she was off and running, sprinting in and out of people on the clogged sidewalk to reach the front of the building. A man in SWAT gear stepped up to block her way.

"Can't go inside, lady. There's a bomb threat."

"I'm a cop." A cop without a badge to flash at him.

"Sure you are." He looked over her street clothes.

"She's with me." Reggie's deep voice made her whirl, and she hurried off with her partner.

"Fill me in," she demanded.

He did, in as few words as possible. Bomb threats made to the court and another civilian target, people to protect. No explosives had been found as of yet, which had the Air Force looking to the skies, but the cops and feds were scrambling, trying to find out which was the real threat or if it really was both. The bomb squads were in the trenches right now.

What was happening? The world was going insane.

"What can I do?" she asked.

"We've already got everybody in the building corralled into one area. Problem is, we've got felons inside on trial. We have to get the court workers and civilians out safely and make sure the felons are evacuated under guard."

"Reg, I need a weapon."

He stared at her. "I thought you always have a concealed carry."

"I did… until the parking lot incident. I haven't carried a weapon since."

"Shit. I'll give you my backup, but I don't like being without. Let's go."

197

As Avery followed her partner into the building, she tossed a look up at the sky. Somewhere Jess was out there, deep in his own brand of danger. She offered up a prayer that they'd both return home safe.

* * * * *

"Jess, what are we lookin' at with this Moreno guy? What is he capable of?" Cav's voice came from over his shoulder.

They were grounded just short of their destination, their orders to pause their mission long enough to get a bead on what was happening. Sully was on the horn with Downs, and the rest of the guys sat on edge, prepared to jump at the first order.

Jess looked at each of his team. Linc and Lennon wore twin expressions of anger and worry. Woody had torn off his helmet and was turning it in his hands, over and over, while staring into space. Cav had his legs braced wide, his posture loose, but Jess knew he was ready to pounce.

Sully turned his back to them, and suddenly he let out a rough, "Goddammit!"

They all stared at their captain.

Sully spun back to the group and swept his gaze over them. "Downs just gave word that there are bomb threats going up in Austin. Two verified targets so far, and a few calls they think are copycat reports but have to be investigated. Every law officer is on the job. Bomb units on scene, and buildings being

198

evacuated and streets cleared. As of now, not a single explosive has been located."

Jesus. Madison.

Every law officer on the job – Avery.

Jess suddenly felt as if he'd burst into flames with the worry hitting him square in the chest. Loving was going to kill him.

Had Avery been called to duty, despite her current state? If they were all hands on deck, it was possible.

Just as quickly as the thought popped into his mind, he felt a surge of pride in her. If anybody threatened his badass woman, he'd receive a round or two in the heart. She wasn't going to take any threat sitting down, and she'd prove to the review board just how capable and levelheaded she was.

Jess ground his molars for a moment before speaking. "Moreno knew we were on to him after our visit to Chiapas. He knows who's been intercepting his messages, that we've been listening in. His contacts wouldn't like that. But so far, Moreno hasn't made any strikes of his own, only shared intel." Jess stated facts everybody already knew.

"But…" Jess looked from man to man. "We know he's been traveling into the US through underground channels. He was here when we were at his house in Chiapas. Moreno's deeper into this than just selling intelligence."

Cav spoke up. "The threat in Mexico is a red herring."

Jess nodded. "He's trying to fake us out." Worry flooded him. What if Moreno was striking back at *him*, since he'd been the one intercepting and deciphering his codes? What if Avery had become a target?

"Threats are against the court building and a shopping mall," Sully stated.

"A government target and a public one," Cav noted.

Sully nodded. "Downs ordered us to turn this chopper around and head back."

"And if there is a threat in Mexico?" Woody asked.

"Then Knight Ops is there to cover it. We're going to be on the streets of Austin searching for that fucking Moreno." Sully looked directly at Jess, and he gave a hard nod in return.

It was time.

"They're talking about dispatching Army Rangers from Fort Benning, but it'll take too long. I think we're on our own, team," Sully said.

"Just get us in there," Jess growled.

He prided himself on remaining cool, calm and together when a threat presented itself. But if something had happened to one of his loved ones — or any of their loved ones — he'd never forgive himself for not pulling the trigger on Moreno long before this day.

Chapter Ten

"This building's clear. That's the last man out," Avery stated to Reggie as she watched the felon being led in shackles onto a prison van.

Reggie looked up from the call he'd just taken. "They need us at the mall. They've got too many people to handle over there, and they need some order. Let's go."

Avery followed her partner out of the court building, past bomb squads and K-9 units that were still searching the place. So far, reports hadn't come in about whether or not a bomb had been found inside—but it didn't matter. She'd done her job by getting the people to safety, and now she had another job to do.

The sidewalk was still clogged with pedestrians trying to get home to their families after learning about the threats.

Reaching their cruiser, Reggie jumped behind the wheel.

"I wish I had on my uniform. I feel I'd hold more authority with the crowd."

"Shit, I forgot I've got an extra vest in the back. Put it on."

She reached over the seat to grab it as he pulled into the traffic, using his siren to get the vehicles to part and allow them through. When she looked in the back, all she saw was a vest with an orange stripe.

"That's a traffic cop vest," she said.

Reggie gave her his trademark grin. "That's what you'll be wearin' after the review board reinstates you. At least for a while."

"Screw you," she shot out, but laughed.

He chuckled along with her, the much-needed tension-breaker leaving both of them feeling looser.

The scanner was blowing up but not with dark tales of explosions one would expect. It was injuries among the crowd of people they were all struggling to keep calm and in order.

"Where's your wife right now, Reg?"

"At home." He pushed out a sigh. "I told her not to leave."

"At least she'll be away from all this."

"Yeah. Where's your boyfriend?"

She pressed her lips together. "He's away for his job." She hadn't told Reggie about Jess's work and wouldn't unless Jess was okay with him knowing.

"Good. The fewer people in this city right now, the better."

She didn't know if it was a good thing the Ranger Ops weren't around to deal with these threats. They were far better equipped than many of the agencies on hand were.

A military vehicle rolled through an intersection, and she tracked it with her eyes. "Looks like the government's sent some backup."

"Fuckin-A."

"Think I'm getting my badge back after this?" she asked, mind skipping from topic to topic.

He shot her a look. "If you don't, I plan to walk in there and throw down my badge too. Because a city that can't recognize a good officer when they see one doesn't deserve to have me on its payroll either."

Her heart welled with appreciation of their friendship. "Thanks, Reg."

"Car forty-nine, what is your location?"

Avery grabbed the two-way receiver and gave the closest street address.

"We need you on the scene at the shopping complex."

"We're headed there now."

"Copy that. And Officer Aarons—welcome back."

Too bad all joy at those words was lost in her worry.

As Reggie took a side street to get around traffic, Avery glanced at her phone again. Nothing from Jess.

She swung her head right and left, watching the buildings for signs of smoke that would indicate an explosion.

"Reports coming in," she said, staring at the laptop now.

"Of what?"

"Suspicious case on the lower level of the mall."

The radio broadcast details from all around Austin. A news helicopter had taken to the skies, which only managed to cause mass panic at a school on the outskirts of city limits, which only meant more cops were called over there to calm things down and reassure them all that they were safe.

Avery felt helpless in every sense. All she could do was sit back and listen and pray she and Reggie did some good in all this.

As soon as they neared the destination, city buses were loading those without vehicles. She and Reggie jumped out of the cruiser, in the thick of it, directing people, assisting an old lady into the back of a waiting ambulance where two other elderly people sat.

Avery spun toward where she'd last seen Reggie, and then she spotted the camo uniforms.

Her heart gave a hard lurch.

No, Jess wasn't among those men. He wasn't in the city.

A middle-aged man came up to her screaming that he'd lost his wife somewhere in the chaos and she wasn't answering her phone. Avery was just trying to calm him down, when a cry rang out.

"He's got a gun!"

People hit the ground with arms flung over their heads or ran willy-nilly into the parking lot. A motorcyclist gunned it through the pedestrians on the sidewalk, knocking people aside.

Avery rushed forward, her own weapon drawn. *Please don't let this be a repeat of the parking lot incident.*

She jerked her head left and right, searching for a shooter in the crowd. Reggie was at her side. "That guy looks suspicious. I'm checking him out," he said.

Giving a nod, she shouldered her way through a group of men and saw the flash of steel in someone's hand.

"Stop right there!"

The man took two more steps.

With a flying leap, she hit the guy square in the back, knocking him flat out on the sidewalk. The weapon skittered out of reach, and another officer was on the scene to pick it up.

Using her weight and strength, she nudged the guy's legs apart and flattened him with a knee on his spine. "Arms out to the sides, palms up!" she ordered.

Another cop appeared next to her. Together, they got the guy handcuffed and on his feet.

"I got this, Aarons. Reggie needs you over there."

She handed the guy over to the other police officer. Suddenly, images of Jess filled her mind. When would she see him again? Did he know what was happening here?

She had barely drawn a breath when she heard Reggie calling her name.

"Aarons!"

She spun and then rushed back to where he was ordering people to remain calm and follow directions. Two firemen jumped in to help, and then she couldn't think of Jess anymore.

She had work to do and knew he was out there somewhere, doing the work he loved too.

* * * * *

"Both buildings have been evacuated. The bomb at the mall is a dud." Linc's announcement had Jess looking up.

"That's one down then. What the fuck's happening at the court?"

"We've got orders to head there now," Sully said.

The guys gathered around the chopper that had just put down. Colonel Downs had a van at the ready for them, and they piled inside.

Being in their home city with their loved ones so close had each of them quiet and drawn into his own thoughts. Jess hoped to hell his daughter and Avery were safe. His chest was tight with worry, but he tried to shake it off and focus on what was ahead.

Sully turned in his seat to look back at Jess. "We're setting you up with computer systems and will proceed into the court building without you. We need you on Moreno."

"Tell me where and I'm there."

Minutes counted down slowly, and Jess's mind wandered over all he knew of Moreno. There was more to the man. He had to be a pivot point, calling the shots for at least some of these terrorist cells. But Jess had a feeling he might have created his own group of followers. A man like Moreno fed on his power. It might have once been enough for him to know a single phone call from him would have a ringleader dropping everything to speak to him. But he'd want more, and to get it, he'd need his own group of men.

Jess needed hooked up to a headset—now. He also wanted access to the past month's worth of conversations between Moreno and his friends, as well as the codes he'd recently cracked. There must be something he was missing.

"This is you, man," Sully said as the van came to a stop.

Jess looked at his team. "Godspeed."

"We've still got communications with you, and we'll be right next door in the court. Focus on your work, and we'll focus on ours. Got it?" Sully's tone was no-nonsense, and Jess was ready.

He nodded and opened the door to find Colonel Downs and two intelligence agents he'd worked with before standing there. Jess went with them, and the van rolled away, a man short.

Jess couldn't think of that right now. "Get me into a headset," he told Downs.

"This way. We're set up and an agent is already dialed in." Downs gave him a sharp glance.

"Moreno?" Jess asked.

"He's silent."

"Fuck."

"Yeah. But if anybody can find where he's at and his activity, it's you."

First he'd been told he was too close to Moreno, and now that was a good thing. He shook his head as he followed the agents and Downs into an office that had been commandeered as their headquarters. Desks had been cleared and computer systems in place.

Jess took a seat immediately and snatched up a headset. For a few minutes, information was scattered. He was hearing police reports of two felons who'd escaped the court during the ruckus of evacuating. They'd believed them to be accounted for, but now realized they were in the wind. Authorities were on the manhunt right now, and he could only think of Avery somewhere out there.

No sooner had he thought this when Cav's voice projected into his ear. "Man, I just saw your girlfriend."

"What?" Jess clenched his fists on the desk. "Where?"

"She's here at the court, part of the search for the escaped convicts."

"Jesus Christ." Now that he knew Avery's whereabouts, he didn't know if he wanted her anywhere near it. And the Municipal Court had a bomb they hadn't yet located, and that put Avery in a path of danger.

"She's okay, Jess. She says she loves you." Cav made a kissy noise.

That ripped a laugh from his lips. "Thanks, Cav."

Intelligence began to trickle in alongside reports. He analyzed the source of a call between one of the men known to be connected with Moreno. The chatter increased, and he and the other agents were working hard to decipher it all. Jess's mind was verging on the point of overload. He passed one call that seemed less important off to another agent.

Downs paced back and forth, but Jess ignored him, tuned into what he was listening to.

With an ear on a conversation, he stared at the last message they'd intercepted from Moreno. Now that Jess had broken the code, he was able to clearly see it. But maybe there was another layer, something he'd missed the first time around, a message that told of the threats to Austin, that might have been avoided if Jess had taken more time...

His mind was torn between the Spanish in his ear and the words on the paper, when it hit him.

Hand shaking, he lifted the pen and scribbled the words underneath the ones he'd already deciphered from the message days ago.

He got to his feet. "Colonel Downs."

He halted mid-pace and strode to Jess. He put the paper into Downs's hand. "This points to Moreno. It's as I suspected when we discovered he'd been entering the US. He's not just a middleman—he's heading this group."

Downs read the message and his head snapped up, gaze piercing Jess. "Do you know where he is?"

"In the US, sir. I believe he's in Austin executing this plan right now, and the strike mentioned in Mexico is a dead end to throw us off his tail. He's taken our interference personal—we've..." he mulled words on his tongue to describe Moreno's mindset, "embarrassed him. He believed his codes uncrackable, and we've wounded his pride. This is all a warning." He waved a hand toward the windows and the city beyond that was under threat.

"Monet. Someone is on here asking for you." The agent tapped her headset.

Jess's heart slammed his chest wall, thoughts of Avery thick in his mind. He dropped to his seat again and switched channels.

It wasn't Cav telling him that Avery had been hurt, thank God.

It was Moreno himself.

Chapter Eleven

Reggie turned to Avery, his face grim as the report came in.

The felons had brained one of the prison guards with a heavy bookend, dragged his unconscious body into a coat closet and taken his weapon. Which meant the manhunt for two armed and dangerous escaped convicts was on.

Avery and Reggie were to remain where they were, on patrol outside the Municipal Court, keeping everybody well away from the building while the bomb unit worked to deactivate the explosives they'd finally found on-site.

She felt tired and grubby, and if she thought too long on Jess, she'd add heart palpitations to that mix, so she shoved thoughts firmly away.

Several feet off, Reggie stood like a brick wall, prohibiting the press, which was still trying to fight their way through to question authorities about the explosives, at bay. At least the damn news chopper had been grounded.

So far, most of the problems had come from panic and the pure stupidity of the public. Thank God nobody had actually been injured from explosions, and the city blocks surrounding the areas were mostly cleared.

"The hospital's on overload," Reggie said. "So many people hurt from being trampled. Delilah was called in as triage nurse."

Avery nodded. "At least you know where she is."

He compressed his lips and nodded. "When will you hear from your man?"

Avery's heart leaped at the thought of him. After seeing the van roll up and the Ranger Ops team hitting the sidewalk in full gear a little bit ago, she'd nearly dropped over with shock. Then she hadn't seen Jess and had taken off running to them.

Cav had intercepted her, taken the time to talk to her and fill her in on Jess's role. He was somewhere nearby, working on intelligence. She wished to hell she could see his face, just to make sure he was all right. So many times she'd seen him return home bruised and battered, bleeding even.

Of course she knew his work was dangerous. But she'd feel better if he was with the rest of his team. Together, they were an unstoppable unit.

"Holy shit! There's our man!" An officer took off running.

She and Reggie looked up, assessing the situation in a blink. She took off sprinting, Reggie a step behind. A man ducked behind a building, his prison yellow clothing sticking out like a beacon.

She powered faster, pumping her arms. She needed to catch this guy and stop the manhunt, which would free up officers out searching for him instead of protecting their city.

Her burst of speed pulled a surprised gasp from Reggie behind her. "You're faster than you were, Aarons."

All that training had done some good then. Now if only the other steps she'd taken to get back her badge were just as successful, she'd be a happy woman.

Weapon drawn, she got the convict in her sights. "I got a shot!"

"Take it!"

Here it was. The parking lot scene flashed into her mind. She hadn't made a mistake then and she wasn't now either.

She aimed and fired. The man fell, and his fellow escapee threw himself forward, striking a huge, heavy sign outside the door of a business. Avery jumped out of the way in the nick of time, but she heard Reggie holler.

The other cops were upon them, two jumping on the man she'd just shot down and three more flattening the other convict onto the pavement.

Avery jerked her head around, looking for Reggie. When she saw him lying beneath the wood and metal sign, her heart gave a lurch. Lunging forward, she was a hundred percent totally prepared for a rescue.

Reggie lay twisted to the side, his leg bent at an odd angle.

She reached for his neck and felt for his pulse.

His eyes popped open. "I'm not dying, woman. You don't need to use that CPR bullshit on me."

"I need an ambulance over here," she called into her walkie-talkie as her partner glared up at her.

"I'll be fine. Just call ahead and tell Delilah that she's gonna be seeing me real soon."

"Reggie, just stay calm. You're bleeding and I don't want you going into shock." Avery noted the bone fragments projecting through his upper thigh. "Lie back now and relax. The medics will only take a minute."

"Call Delilah."

"I will. I'll tell her not to worry, okay? That her husband's just as much of a stubborn ass as ever."

He flashed a weak grin. "Guess you'll be on traffic cop duty by yourself now, Aarons. Looks like I'll be laid up a while."

* * * * *

Jess was aware of utter silence around him.

"This is Special Operative Jess Monet on the line."

"I know you've been listening to my calls," the man said in his heavily accented English.

216

"Moreno. You know we don't negotiate with terrorists. But it's not too late to do the right thing."

"I have done the right thing." He was gaining confidence that he had the upper hand here, but Jess had to keep him off-balance.

Sweat broke out on his brow, and a bead slithered between his shoulder blades. What he was about to say would lure out the worst in Moreno, but it had to be done.

"Why did your wife take her life?"

Jess's question was met with complete silence. He waited for the telltale click on his end that meant the line was disconnected. But he never heard it.

"My wife has nothing to do with this."

"Sure, she does. She took her life because of what you were involved in, didn't she? After that first bombing back in Mexico City, she found out what you were doing and decided she couldn't remain married to a man like you."

"You know nothing of my wife or my life," he bit off.

"Don't I? I've read reports. I know she came from a small town, she grew up poor. She married you for love, but you turned quick, didn't you? You had to make money in some way, and you turned to selling intelligence. What I want to know is who else is involved? I want the names of the men who follow you."

217

"I refuse to discuss any of this. It is too late to stop it, and all your people are in peril."

"You think you can lead these men, that they're loyal to you. You're wrong. They aren't your friends and wouldn't bat an eye at seeing you dead. Or your children."

"Listen, you *bastardo*." Evil seeped into his words. "It is you who will be dead."

"Know what I think?" Jess went on.

"No, I do not care to."

"I believe there's a bigger target, that these bomb threats were a diversion for something larger. You know what it is."

A laugh followed, and Jess brought his fingers up to pinch the bridge of his nose. That code… Was there a third layer? Perhaps what he'd given Downs just now wasn't the entire message.

"Moreno." Jess pitched his voice low. "Your children, Lalia and Brayan."

"You know nothing of my children."

"But I do. I know they favor *torta de tres leches*. And you gave Brayan a new bicycle for his ninth birthday. Lalia is growing up so fast, interested in music and wearing her hair different."

More silence.

"Moreno. I've got a daughter as well. She's growing up and I haven't been there enough for her either. Both of us still have time. Father to father, tell

218

me how to stop this." Jess's words poured out in Moreno's Spanish tongue.

"I cannot do that."

"Your children deserve to grow up with their father. And not the father you have been these past years since Maria's death either—a good man. Now tell me, Moreno, do you have the power in your hands to stop this attack?"

Another laugh, this one dry and brittle.

"Moreno. If you stop this, we will provide safety for you and your family, even your caretaker and your cook Juanita."

He sucked in a breath.

"We will get you all to safety and see you're protected. New names, new lives."

"We don't need any of that. We don't need your help," he rasped.

Jess was getting to him, he knew by the strain in his tone. "But Maria would want it. Isn't this what you should have given your wife before she found herself trapped with a man who was choosing the wrong side and took her own life?"

Moreno let out a few whispered words that Jess couldn't exactly make out.

He opened his mouth to press on him some more, but Moreno cut off.

The line was dead.

Jess shot to his feet, hands fisted at his sides. "Someone get me the last ten communications from Moreno," he barked out.

A flurry of activity took place, as the other agents typed away. In moments, they had everything up on Jess's computer monitors. He stared at each. "C'mon, you son of a bitch. Show me what you're hiding."

The letters and numbers scrambled in his brain, but one broke free. Then another.

"Jesus Christ." He looked up at Colonel Downs, who hovered over him, forehead wrinkled in strain.

"What is it, Monet?"

"It isn't what's on these screens. It's what Moreno whispered just a bit ago. He was talking to someone else, but I caught it."

"If you can put a stop to this, I'm listening," Downs said.

Jess stood. "It's the airport. Stop all flights coming in and going out and start evacuation immediately."

* * * * *

The waiting room of the hospital where Reggie had been taken was packed wall to wall with people. Reggie's wife Delilah clutched a paper cup of coffee she never took a sip of. It was just something to occupy her hand while they waited for news on Reggie, who was in surgery.

Ever since Avery had heard his compound fracture had been critically close to his femoral artery, she'd felt like she could use something much stronger than coffee. But she was trying to hold it together for his wife's sake. As a nurse, Delilah knew far too much about the dangerous situation her husband was in.

Avery rested her hand on Delilah's shoulder, making her look up. "I'm going to step outside and try to make a phone call, okay? I'll be right back."

She nodded, and Avery moved away. As she looked at the faces of the people who were waiting to hear about the condition or whereabouts of their loved ones, she felt very small for worrying about her own life. The whole mess with the review and the board who couldn't get their act together and just make the decision on her case seemed so inconsequential in the face of… well, all of it.

Heart burning out of her chest with fear for the man she loved, Avery couldn't bring herself to care if she lost her badge anymore.

She stepped into the night. Lights from the hospital cast streaks across the pavement. The emergency entrance was still jam-packed with ambulances and squad cars. She moved away from it all, down the sidewalk until she reached a solitary lot where the physicians parked.

Bringing her phone up, she saw the battery was nearly dead. It was the longest day of her life, but she couldn't breathe until she heard Jess's voice.

Ever since news had hit that the airport had been the real target all along and that a small private aircraft carrying enough explosives to take out thousands of people traveling at the time had been discovered on the runway, she'd known exactly where Jess would be.

She ran her fingers through her disheveled hair and dialed his cell. Of course it didn't go through. He didn't have his personal phone on him.

Tilting her head back, she looked at the clouds, where the Air Force was patrolling their skies. She still couldn't breathe easy even knowing they were being watched over. Not with Reggie in surgery... and Jess out of arms' reach.

Just then, her phone buzzed, and she saw the number belonging to Madison's mother. She yanked the phone to her ear.

"Madison?"

"Yes, it's me. My dad just called me. He's safe. He's all right!" Her young voice projected into Avery's ear.

Suddenly, Avery's knees felt wobbly. She thought she might sit down hard right there in the parking lot, but she braced a hand against the nearest car to hold herself upright.

"I just heard from him. He's—"

Her phone blipped.

Avery drew it away from her ear to stare at the screen. "I think he's calling me now! I'll talk to you as soon as I'm off the phone with him, okay, sweetie?"

Avery ended the call and switched over. She didn't even open her mouth to say hello, when Jess's voice projected into her ear.

"Baby."

"Oh my God. Jess!" Tears sprang to her eyes.

His voice thickened. "Fuck, it's good to hear your voice."

"I know. Where are you? Are you safe?"

"Yes. It's over. We're en route back to HQ. Where are you?"

"The hospital."

"Shit. Are you all right? What happened?"

"It's my partner, Reggie. There was an accident, and he's in surgery."

"Jesus Christ. Thank God you're okay, though."

Her heart ached to be with him.

"I have to get back inside and comfort his wife. Until Reggie's out of surgery and I know he's okay, I can't leave the hospital."

"I'll come to you."

"You don't have to. You must be exhausted and—"

"I'll come to you," he stated again.

She pushed out a teary sigh. "I'll be waiting. I'm so glad you're all right and that this is over. Please tell me it's really over."

"It is."

Her throat closed off. "Moreno?"

There was a beat of silence before Jess spoke. "I did my job."

Her throat closed. They both had.

"Gotta run, baby. I'll meet you at the hospital."

"Jess, before you go."

"Yeah?"

"I love you so much."

* * * * *

The condo was dead silent, dark and the perfect place to seduce his lover.

Avery traced her fingers over Jess's brow, her heart glowing in her eyes. He cupped her beautiful face in his hands, leaning near to let his lips hover just over hers.

Her bare flesh seared against his, her nipples hard peaks against his chest and her toned abs cradling his hard cock. It hadn't gone down in hours and hours, and he could no longer chalk it up to the adrenaline rush of battle. He just couldn't stop wanting her.

Catching her lips beneath his, he closed his eyes and inhaled the sweet scent of her shampoo and pure woman.

"Wanton woman," he whispered between nibbling kisses. "Needy woman." He pulled away and lifted her, laying her out on the mattress.

She stared up at him with desire burning on her face. Without hesitating, Jess slipped down between her thighs and dragged his tongue over her soaking pussy folds.

"Delicious woman."

She shuddered.

Slipping a finger into her tight sheath, he lapped a path up to her clit and sucked on the small, hard nub. Her hips bucked off the bed, and he clutched onto her hip with his free hand, holding her in place while he kissed every inch of her.

She cried out when he eased his finger out of her pussy and thrust it back in. Her insides clamped down on his digit, and his cock responded with a hard jerk. Pre-cum oozed from the tip to wet the sheets under him, and it felt like it'd been months since he'd had her beneath him, when it had only been an hour at most. Still, he could wait to sink into her and fuck her the way he wanted to.

First he wanted her screaming his name.

Swirling her hips, she ground her clit over his tongue. He sucked it between his lips and pressed his tongue down lightly. She rocked her head back on a cry.

Watching her was the most erotic thing he'd ever done. He damn well wanted to see her this way, in the throes of ecstasy, every day for the rest of their lives.

He plunged his finger into her core again. She grasped his head and shoved him down for more even as he tormented her with long swaths of his tongue over her entire pussy.

"I'm... close," she rasped out.

She didn't need to tell him—he knew what those small squeaks she made meant.

And the way her nipples darkened to a deep rose color.

Releasing her hip, he reached up her body and thumbed one nipple. She clenched and released on his finger, under his tongue.

Before she burst with her orgasm, he pushed to his knees, yanked her hips up and sank deep.

Her channel was so fucking hot, so mind-blowing. He growled with lust as he thrust into her. She rose to meet him, and the sound of their lovemaking fueled him on. He could go on like this forever, he thought.

When she began to quiver, he felt her tongue stroking across his neck. Opening his eyes, he twisted his head to gaze down at her. Then she kissed him, a white-hot meshing of their tongues that sent the first jet of cum up from his balls.

It erupted from him at the same second a throaty groan ripped from her mouth. She clutched his shoulders and levered herself into him as her pussy pulsated around his bare length.

Pleasure blasted his senses. He ran his tongue over hers, a litany of love words playing through his brain, flashing like movie credits. Unreadable, but he knew how he felt about her.

He couldn't live without Avery in his life.

And at the same time, he was afraid to ask her, to make her his.

In the past, his desire to seal the deal had only driven away the women in his life. Sure, Avery was different, but was he?

The final drop of cum spurted into her body, and he managed to brace himself on his elbows though he wanted to collapse, finally sapped.

When he finally broke the kiss and looked into her eyes, he saw love staring right back at him.

This woman *was* different. And he wasn't about to let her get away.

Dropping his forehead to hers, he fought to gain his breath and senses before he spoke. Last thing he wanted was to speak in haste and fuck it all up.

"I don't know how I can have one more orgasm. I think that was the… fifth time tonight?" She panted.

Still joined with her, he searched the depths of her eyes. "Marry me."

Fuck, he'd said that.

He hadn't meant to say that.

Holding his breath, he noticed the stunned look crossing her face and hurried to take it back.

"Hell, I didn't mean that."

Her eyes flew open wider.

"Shit. I did mean it. Fuck!" He separated their bodies and moved to the edge of the bed, lowering his head into his hands. He challenged huge threats and laughed in the face of death. But he was terrified of what he'd just done.

A rustling sound came from behind and a second later, Avery stood in front of him, naked and ripe and the most stunning creature he'd ever seen in his life.

She settled her hands on her hips, head cocked. "Is that all you've got to say to me? You didn't meant that? And fuck?"

He groaned. "I've messed it all up."

"Messed what up?"

"I shouldn't have said the M word. I knew as soon as it slipped out of my mouth, that you'd run."

"You know I'll run from you asking me to marry you," she repeated.

He chanced a look at her face. He couldn't read her. Dammit, being married to a cop would be just as bad as her being married to an operative. Each of them could hide from the other.

Or we can choose to hide nothing at all.

He looked up into her eyes, exposing his feelings to her. Raw and without barriers.

"I want you to be my wife." His voice was gritty.

She stood there a moment. Then her eyes fluttered shut and a tear trickled down her cheek.

He couldn't take it anymore—he grabbed her by the waist and yanked her forward to stand between his knees. "I'm in love with you, and I don't want to live another day without you by my side. I'm probably the absolute worst partner for you. I'm not around a lot. I'll come home late and leave early. I'll miss Christmas and birthdays and New Year's Eve kisses..."

"And so will I." Her words came out thickly. "But I love you, and I don't want to be without you another day either. So..." She shoved him backward. His back hit the bed, and she crawled atop him, still slick and dripping his juices as she straddled him.

With her hands braced on his chest, she stared down into his eyes. "If you won't own up to saying it, I will. Marry me, Jess."

"Oh no. I won't let you outdo me. Marry me, Avery."

A grin flashed across her face, followed by genuine joy and the glow of love. "Yes," she whispered, leaning down to brush her lips over his.

"Yes," he responded to her proposal too. He kissed her right back, sealing both their fates in the thrill of love.

Epilogue

Reggie stumped around Avery's small balcony on his crutches and cast, wielding a spatula. "Let me at those burgers."

She held up her hands. "You should really sit down, Reggie. Take a load off that leg."

"I'm fine, woman. Between you and my wife, I can't get any peace. Do you have any idea how boring it is waiting for this to heal?" He tapped his cast with the spatula.

She leveled a look at him. "Yeah, I actually do."

"At least you could go to the gym and occupy your time. I'm getting cushy sitting around watching daytime TV."

That brought a laugh to her lips. "Tend the burgers, Reg. I'm going inside and check the brisket. Keep those coals hot so I can sear the meat when it comes out of the oven."

"Ohhh yeah, we need all those good grill marks." He shot her a grin, which she returned.

When she entered her kitchen again, it was a packed house. Two more of the Ranger Ops team had joined the party along with their ladies.

She looked around. "Where's Jess gone to now?"

He'd been more secretive than normal lately, and just when she thought he was done showering her with another new present—so far, he'd given her a gold necklace, a bunch of balloons big enough to fill her entire living room, and a sleek new concealed carry holster that fit perfectly along her torso, he vanished again.

"I think Jess went out for a minute."

Shaking her head, Avery just smiled and went about fixing the brisket. When she pulled it from the oven, she could already see the meat was falling apart, and the aroma was mouthwatering.

Cav came to lean over her shoulder. He sniffed deeply and reached for a bit of meat.

She slapped his hand.

"Hey, I don't care if you're going after pork or not. Get away from my girl." Jess's voice filled Avery with happiness. She turned to shoot him a wink and stopped when she saw her mom and dad standing there. Not far off, Madison was talking to another young girl, a friend she'd brought to the party.

"What a surprise!" Avery rushed across the room to embrace both her parents. Then she and Madison air-kissed, something they'd started doing over the past few months since Jess had gotten more involved in his daughter's life.

Avery turned to drink in a long look of her favorite people all crowded in her apartment. "I think

I need a bigger place," she told Jess, reaching up to kiss his jaw.

He brought his arm around her, tugging her close. "That's what I was hoping you'd say."

She searched his eyes. "What do you mean?"

"I want the next party to be at *our* place."

When confusion pinched her brows, he flattened his palm on her spine to bring her a step closer into his arms. "I want you to move in with me. Makes it easier to spend time together... and plan the wedding."

She laughed. "Jess, you're worse than a woman with all the wedding magazines I've seen stuffed in your car."

"Hey, you never can be too involved in this stuff. And I want to be there for you, Avery."

"You're just as busy as I am."

"Exactly. It shouldn't all fall on you to plan. But now that your parents are in town, I was thinking they may want to help us choose a venue. Then a cake."

"Jess! What did you do?"

"I might have set up a few appointments tomorrow. Is that okay?"

She locked her arms around his neck and stared deep into his eyes. "Yes, it is. We have to take advantage of the times we get together."

Cradling her nape, he brushed his lips across her forehead. "That won't get easier. Sure you can deal with marrying a man in my position?"

She cocked a brow. "Think you can deal with marrying a cop?"

A wicked grin spread across his face. He slid his hand down her side. "A sexy as hell cop."

"Hey, Aarons," Reggie called out from the doorway. "Thought you wanted me to keep this grill hot for that brisket?"

Laughing, she pulled free of Jess's arms.

Before she could turn away, he grabbed her hand and a second later, she felt him slide something onto her ring finger.

Gasping, she looked down to see the simple square-cut ring she would have chosen for herself if he'd taken her shopping—modest and minimalistic.

"I've already asked this amazing woman this question, but I wanted all of our friends and family to witness it." Jess's announcement had her puzzled, until he swooped onto one knee.

The entire kitchen exploded into applause. He raised his voice to be heard. "Avery Aarons, I've asked you once, but I'm making it official now in front of everybody we care for. Would you do me the honor of becoming my wife?"

Tipping forward into his outstretched arms, she planted a kiss on him that changed the applause to catcalls and whistles. When they broke apart, she looked into Jess's happy gaze. She knew it reflected her own.

"Baby, I promise I'll keep the fires going between us all our lives."

"You better," she said with a teary sniff.

"Yeah, man, she's got a gun," Cav shot out.

"And she can taze your ass," Sully added.

Avery tipped her face up for Jess's kiss. The brush of his mouth across hers promised so much more... once they were alone. "You're a little too good at surprises. I didn't realize this get-together was actually our engagement party."

He stroked his thumb over her cheek. "You're easier to surprise than you think."

"Oh, so now I'm clueless. Thanks." She pinched his hard backside.

He rumbled a laugh and scooped her up into his arms once more. With his face buried in her hair, he whispered, "You're my everything. Love you, baby."

Turning her mouth to his ear, she whispered a few dirty things she had planned for later after everybody left. When she drew back, his eyes burned for more.

She arched a brow at him. "Maybe I've got a few surprises for you too, Jess."

"I'll kick everyone out."

"Don't you dare! Now grab that brisket before Reggie has a fit, while I go hug my parents and my soon-to-be stepdaughter-slash-bridesmaid."

His eyes glowed, mirroring all the love and joy she felt at this moment. Both of them knew there'd be ups and downs—they'd already lived through some. But together and with a love like theirs, they could overcome all obstacles.

THE END

Em Petrova

Em Petrova was raised by hippies in the wilds of Pennsylvania but told her parents at the age of four she wanted to be a gypsy when she grew up. She has a soft spot for babies, puppies and 90s Grunge music and believes in Bigfoot and aliens. She started writing at the age of twelve and prides herself on making her characters larger than life and her sex scenes hotter than hot.

She burst into the world of publishing in 2010 after having five beautiful bambinos and figuring they were old enough to get their own snacks while she pounds away at the keys. In her not-so-spare time, she is fur-mommy to a Labradoodle named Daisy Hasselhoff.

Find More Books by Em Petrova at

Other Titles by Em Petrova

Ranger Ops
AT CLOSE RANGE
WITHIN RANGE
POINT BLANK RANGE
RANGE OF MOTION
TARGET IN RANGE
OUT OF RANGE

Knight Ops Series
ALL KNIGHTER
HEAT OF THE KNIGHT
HOT LOUISIANA KNIGHT
AFTER MIDKNIGHT
KNIGHT SHIFT
ANGEL OF THE KNIGHT
O CHRISTMAS KNIGHT

Wild West Series
SOMETHING ABOUT A LAWMAN
SOMETHING ABOUT A SHERIFF
SOMETHING ABOUT A BOUNTY HUNTER
SOMETHING ABOUT A MOUNTAIN MAN

Operation Cowboy Series

KICKIN' UP DUST
SPURS AND SURRENDER

The Boot Knockers Ranch Series
PUSHIN' BUTTONS
BODY LANGUAGE
REINING MEN
ROPIN' HEARTS
ROPE BURN
COWBOY NOT INCLUDED

The Boot Knockers Ranch Montana
COWBOY BY CANDLELIGHT
THE BOOT KNOCKER'S BABY
ROPIN' A ROMEO

Country Fever Series
HARD RIDIN'
LIP LOCK
UNBROKEN
SOMETHIN' DIRTY

Rope 'n Ride Series
BUCK
RYDER

RIDGE

WEST

LANE

WYNONNA

Rope 'n Ride On Series

JINGLE BOOTS

DOUBLE DIPPIN

LICKS AND PROMISES

A COWBOY FOR CHRISTMAS

LIPSTICK 'N LEAD

The Dalton Boys

COWBOY CRAZY Hank's story

COWBOY BARGAIN Cash's story

COWBOY CRUSHIN' Witt's story

COWBOY SECRET Beck's story

COWBOY RUSH Kade's Story

COWBOY MISTLETOE a Christmas novella

COWBOY FLIRTATION Ford's story

COWBOY TEMPTATION Easton's story

COWBOY SURPRISE Justus's story

COWGIRL DREAMER Gracie's story

COWGIRL MIRACLE Jessamine's Story

Single Titles and Boxes

STRANDED AND STRADDLED
LASSO MY HEART
SINFUL HEARTS
BLOWN DOWN
FALLEN
FEVERED HEARTS
WRONG SIDE OF LOVE

Club Ties Series
LOVE TIES
HEART TIES
MARKED AS HIS
SOUL TIES
ACE'S WILD

Firehouse 5 Series
ONE FIERY NIGHT
CONTROLLED BURN
SMOLDERING HEARTS

The Quick and the Hot Series
DALLAS NIGHTS
SLICK RIDER
SPURRED ON